WHERE MORE THAN THE WINDOWS ARE STEAMY

A Prince for Christmas

A Snowy Hollow Novel

Alexa B. James
&
Lauren M. Phelps

A Prince for Christmas
Copyright © 2021 Alexa B. James
Large Print Edition

Cover Design by Everly Yours

ISBN-13: 978-1-955913-88-1

For everyone who looks forward to setting up the tree, who gets happy when Christmas songs start playing on the radio, and who loves putting on fuzzy socks and watching Hallmark movies as much as I do.

CHAPTER 1

What a lousy day for rain. I huddled back into the doorway as I tried to tuck my books and papers under my coat, getting ready to make a run for it. Unfortunately, the Wayward Wings was a full three blocks from the building I'd just finished class in, and the weatherman this morning hadn't mentioned needing an umbrella by afternoon. I took a deep breath and sprinted down the wet sidewalk, telling myself that it was just as good for me as time at the gym.

By the time I pushed through the broad wooden door that opened directly into the main bar area, I was thoroughly drenched, gasping for breath, and shivering from the cold. I was also late, as my phone alarm had been announcing for a good ten minutes.

I glanced around the room, which was already half full, mainly students unwinding after class with a sprinkling of older folks, the usual after-work crowd. No sign of Mr. McGregor. I peered into the dining room, but didn't see him there, either.

If I punched in and looked busy, he wouldn't notice my lateness until he checked the timecards. Trying to brush my hair out of my eyes as I dashed toward the timeclock behind the bar caused my books to shift in my arms, and when I crashed into a customer, they all went flying. I only managed to keep from falling on my butt by grasping at the collar of the man's coat, and a few choice words escaped me.

"Well, pardon me. I didn't realize I was in the fast lane." The man's deep, smoky voice and foreign accent snapped me out of my grumpiness, and I stepped back to take stock. It was more than worth it. He was almost a head taller than me, with startling blue eyes and a smile that seemed a little mocking. Then there was that accent—Australian? Or maybe English? My Montana ears couldn't tell, but it made him stand out, that's for sure.

Everything about him stood out, to be honest. He looked athletic, but not like the farm boys from back home.

His physique seemed to come from an expensive gym, not log-rolling or wrangling cattle or shoveling snow.

All in all, he looked downright delicious… And totally out of place in the Wayward Wings. I decided my best move in this embarrassing moment was a little bravado.

I met his eyes, took a deep breath, and let my bartending instincts take over. "This is Boseman, Honey. We don't have a fast lane," I said with my best leave-a-tip smile. "It was my fault. I was running late and didn't pay attention."

"We'd better do something about these books before they get trampled," he said, arching a brow.

He bent to start picking up books and papers, and I quickly joined in. When he handed them to me, I couldn't help but notice his masculine hands and manicured nails. I'd never seen a man with such nice hands. I curled my fingers around the books to hide my own hands, knowing they had ink stains from taking notes and hadn't seen a nail file all semester.

"Thanks so much," I gushed, trying to cover my embarrassment. "I'm not usually this clumsy." I edged towards the time clock, ready to end the awkward encounter.

My progress was halted by a heavy hand on my shoulder. Damn. There was Mr. McGregor, staring at me with his usual scowl. I responded with an apologetic smile. "Sorry I'm late, Sir. The rain...." I trailed off as the additional wrinkle to his brow let me know my apology was falling on deaf ears.

"Excuses, excuses," he grumbled. "You young people always have one. You think you can show up when you want, waltz in here with another sob story, and I'll keep on paying you."

"The weatherman didn't predict rain today," I offered, unsure whether the truth or a penitent look would appease him today.

He made a sound that was somewhere between a cough and a growl. "I'm not going to dock you, but you'll make up for it today."

I braced myself for the full lecture, but Mr. McGregor seemed to have something else on his mind. It couldn't be worse than listening to his opinions on young people today, most of which had nothing to do with me. I worked hard for every penny I had, trying not to go into debt for the tuition my partial scholarship didn't cover. I even worked during summer and Christmas breaks at the farm. My parents paid me what I could have earned in Boseman as a bartender because they needed the help and because they knew I needed to go home in the summers. It was hard enough spending nine months away from the mountains.

I fought down a bit of resentment toward my surly boss. I was only late on Thursdays, and that was because my class always ran late. McGregor could've adjusted my schedule, but he'd refused to let me start my shift half an hour later.

I'd heard that lecture a time or two.

"You think the customers should wait for a half-hour? In my bar, without anyone to serve them a drink? Do you have any idea what it costs just to keep this place open, with or without customers?" He'd shaken his head in disgust. I knew it was all a show for my benefit because the day server would have been happy for the extra money.

Sometimes I wondered if I would've been better off if I'd chosen some kind of agriculture major or even veterinary school, but the truth was, I couldn't stand the sight of blood, and I couldn't imagine killing an animal, even though it might be the most merciful thing. And I really couldn't imagine spending my life running my parents' farm, despite the fact that I loved them dearly and even loved working on a farm.

My first love was literature, and from a young age, I'd dreamed of passing my love of the written word on to others. That meant teaching in a university somewhere, despite the disappointment my parents had expressed.

Anyway, McGregor really wasn't so bad. His curmudgeon act was mostly just that—an act. When Ben's grandma was sick and he had to go home during finals, McGregor actually helped work the dining room and fill in where he was needed. In truth, the tips were good, the hours worked for a student, and even though my boss was a bit of a pain, I wouldn't mind keeping this job until I graduated.

I gave Mr. McGregor a conciliatory smile. "How am I going to make up for it?" I asked, expecting to hear that I was assigned to stay late for clean-up at the end of the night, which was fine. I always seemed to be short of money, so staying late wasn't too much of a punishment.

"You're going to be training the new guy tonight. And for the next week."

"Oh, Lord," I muttered. I didn't mind helping out, but I sure hoped it wasn't someone completely hopeless like the last couple people McGregor had tried to hire. Pickings were slim around the holidays, with most students going home. It was an odd time to hire for the same reason.

"Ben's grandmother is in bad shape again, and he's transferring to a school close to home," my boss said. "In fact, he left today."

"That's too bad. I'll miss him." That was very true. Ben was easy to work with and good at his job, though I didn't know him too well. "So where is this new guy?"

"You just ran him over." Amusement crept into Mr. McGregor's voice, although he didn't let himself smile.

The stranger, who had appeared beside us, wasn't as stingy with his smile. He flashed perfect, blinding white teeth at me as he stuck out a hand. "Nick Lancaster. Pleased to meet you."

Damn. He had a stunningly good smile. The kind of smile that would make a weaker woman's heart flutter and bring a blush to her cheeks. Fortunately, I was a sensible girl, and I wasn't one to be taken in by a gorgeous smile. If my cheeks were feeling hot, it was from windburn on my way here.

"Emily Miller," I said as I shifted the books again to shake his hand. His big, warm hand wrapped around mine, his fingers long and strong, with those beautifully kept nails. I tried to imagine those hands in a sink full of hot, soapy water to keep from imagining them someplace on my body… And couldn't quite get there. "So, what position will you be working?"

Did that sound sexy? Crap.

"That's up to Mr. McGregor," Nick replied, arching a brow.

Gah, why was he so handsome? My cheeks were going to be windburned all night at this rate.

"I want him to be able to fill in where he's needed up here, just like you," McGregor said. "Teach him everything about front of the house, starting from the bottom and working up. Tonight you can show him the dining room, since we're short there."

"Really? Who didn't show?"

"Earl."

I felt my eyes widen. "Earl? Again?"

"Damn kid, says he has the stomach flu."

I stared at Nick, all six-foot-something of perfectly cut lines in a blazer that looked custom fit for his broad shoulders and slacks that looked like they were also made to hug him just right. Between that and his clean hands and refined manners and accent, he wouldn't last a minute. Earl was the busboy. How was I supposed to make this tall hunk of privilege work as a busboy? I tried not to grimace.

"Who else is in the dining room?" I asked, hoping I could do a little shuffling and give Nick an easier start to the restaurant business. Somehow, I suspected this would be his first exposure to it.

"No one. Marcy has finals, and it's Glenda's turn to bartend." We rotated the dining room, cocktail waitress and bartender jobs, because the bartender always made the most in tips. Mr. McGregor thought it was fairer than pooling tips because, according to him, pooling favored the laziest server.

We were two short tonight, with only a clueless new guy to fill in. Oh lordy me. Work was going to test my nerves tonight.

CHAPTER 2

I swallowed down a wave of dismay. I hoped it didn't show. Nick Lancaster looked like he belonged in a stockbroker's office, or maybe an expensive supper club, not a run-down college hang-out. There had to be a story there, but I quickly put that out of my mind.

I had enough problems staying on task as it was, without the distraction of a shamefully handsome trainee. Taking a deep breath, I turned to him and smiled, trying to give him the benefit of the doubt. "I guess it's just you and me tonight. Have you ever bussed tables?"

His blank stare told me more than I wanted to know. "Bussed tables?" he asked carefully, looking like I was speaking a foreign language.

Oh, good grief. He didn't even know what I was talking about. I wondered briefly what I could do to get even with old McGregor for dumping this newbie in my lap.

"Cleared them," I said, making an effort to not sound impatient. "A customer comes in, the hostess seats them, the waitress takes their order and serves them, then the busboy removes the dishes. Except we only have you and me for the entire dining room tonight."

He blinked at me, realization seeming to dawn. "That leaves us in quite a pickle, doesn't it?" he asked, his accent making it hard not to laugh when he used that expression.

I blew a wet strand of hair out of my face and tried to stay businesslike. "We don't have a hostess, so I'll be seating them. You'll be clearing dishes. I'll be taking their orders and serving food, and one of us will be serving drinks, whoever is less busy."

"Sounds like we've got it covered, then." He seemed agreeable, but I was pretty sure he had not a clue what I was talking about.

I took a deep breath. "Have you ever worked in a restaurant before?"

He gave a little shrug. "No."

"Okay. Here's what we're going to do." I found a place to set down my soggy books, then took his hand. Big mistake. It was warm and huge and disturbingly comforting, and instead of leading him through this stressful night, I pictured a stroll down a beach somewhere tropical...

I pulled my hand away as if I'd been burned. "Come with me. We're going to work through this together, and you'll be fine," I lied.

Meanwhile, I was trying not to panic. We would not be fine for one single minute. A brief survey of the dining room told me that, at the moment, everyone had their food, but there were five tables needing to be cleared. I handed Nick an apron—bussing tables was hard on street clothes, and his looked like they cost a pretty penny—and directed him to get the dish cart and follow me. Table by table, we loaded the dirty dishes onto bins on the rolling cart. Nick seemed to take surprising pleasure in clearing the dishes. When at last we pushed the cart into the kitchen, where Eddy, whose face was so freckled it was hard to figure out which spots were acne and which were freckles, was washing dishes,

Nick gave him the same blinding smile and formal handshake he'd given me.

"I'm quite properly amazed," he said. "Who knew all this went on behind the scenes at a restaurant?"

Eddy gave him a funny look and started grabbing the plastic tubs of dishes.

Seemingly dissuaded from further conversation, Nick turned to me. "What next, Boss?"

Something about that tone made me bristle. Arrogance was my first thought, but maybe it was just that foreign accent. I got the feeling this was all a big game to him. Was he kidding, or baiting me, or was he serious?

I gave him a brittle smile. "Rinse and repeat for the rest of the night," I said. "And if you run out of tables to clear, start wiping down the ones you've cleared with one of those disinfectant rags, then put down the paper placemats, and the wrapped napkin-silverware bundles."

His perfect eyebrows drew together. "Shouldn't there be someone besides us to do that?"

I tried to hold on to my patience. It didn't work.

"There should be," I said with a sigh. "But they didn't show up. The customers didn't get the memo and came anyway. That means it's you and me. Do you have a problem with that?"

"Of course not, Sergeant," His mocking salute irritated me further, but I took a deep breath to keep from snapping.

Who did this guy think he was?

"So, where are the silverware sets and placemats?" His question calmed me down a bit, since he was actually helping despite the attitude.

I showed him where they were stored and how to set a table and then scrambled to take orders. The night was no busier than was usual for a Wednesday night, but with only two people doing the job of four, it would have been an utterly exhausting night even with Ben there. Instead, I had a new guy who had no experience and no clue. To be fair, he worked hard, but I had to train him as well as doing the job of two others, and by the end of the shift, all I wanted to do was go home, shower the smell of hot-wings from my body, and pass out. Instead, I had this trainee to deal with.

Mr. McGregor, trusting me far more than he should, had taken off after the dinner crowd, when only a few stragglers remained in the dining area. He'd instructed me to close up and have Nick help me.

As if Nick knew enough to help anyone with anything in the restaurant.

Still, he'd been a trooper and a quick learner, I had to admit. Once I showed him how to keep the tables emptied, disinfected, and re-dressed with placemats, silverware, and napkins, he'd kept the dining room clean all evening. He'd even helped me with seating new guests a couple of times.

Finally, closing time arrived. During the week, the restaurant closed at ten, the bar at eleven. With Nick's help, I had the dining room ready for the lunch crowd by the time the bar was ready to close down. The bar was often nastier than the dining room, because drinkers tended to get messy after a few drinks.

I blamed my exhaustion for the next unkind thought to pop into my head.

Maybe I'll get lucky, and it'll be too messy for fancy Nick to show up again.

I'd been making bets with myself all night about when he'd admit he'd had enough and walk out on me. I couldn't believe he'd stuck around this long. I knew it wasn't really fair to him. It wasn't his fault that we were short staffed or even that he was new. But it wasn't my fault either—or that I'd gotten stuck training a new guy on top of running the front of the place nearly on my own.

Still, if I was feeling frazzled, I couldn't imagine how it must feel to be the new guy walking into this madhouse.

To my surprise, and a bit of guilt at my less than charitable thoughts, Nick stuck around and helped empty and wipe down the bar area. I gently encouraged the few hangers-on to take their drunken selves on down the road. As I patted one half-drunk regular on the shoulder and confirmed that he was on foot and only had a few blocks to go, I noticed Nick watching intently.

When the last patrons had been sent home, some by cajoling, a couple with my well-practiced stern look, I turned to Nick. "So, that's a fairly typical night at the Wayward Wings. Shall I tell Mr. McGregor that you're just not interested?"

I didn't know what answer I was hoping for. His ignorance was as irritating as his arrogance, but I had to admit that he did give the place a little class. And something yummier than chicken wings for the ladies to drool over.

"Why would you do that? I find it fascinating." Nick looked perfectly serious, even though he'd spent the evening on the run, trying to be a person-and-a-half as he bussed tables, set them, and occasionally seated people and ran drinks out.

"Well, I've never heard this job described quite that way, but I'm glad you enjoyed it."

"Indeed I did, Emily," he said, holding my gaze for a second.

I shoved down a little wave of pleasure at the sound of my name rolling off his sophisticated tongue. No one had ever said my name quite like that before. It made me feel as fancy as he sounded.

"So, uh, you'll be back tomorrow?" I asked.

"I will." He slid his hands into his pockets, looking down at me in a way that was eighter haughty or English. It was hard to tell with only my small-town experience. I was from Snowy Hollow, Montana, and let's just say we didn't get a lot of foreigners. This was the big city for us.

"Is that okay with you?" he asked.

"Oh, well, it's not really up to me," I said with a shrug, like I didn't give a hoot.

My pulse was telling a different story.

*

True to his word, Nick showed up the next day for his shift, and for every shift he was scheduled after that. Mr. McGregor seemed to have decided we made a good team, because our shifts seemed to always coincide.

Working with him created a dilemma. Not only was he a quick study, he was more than willing to pull his weight, even when other staff didn't show up, which happened often in a college town. Although he wasn't big on sharing personal details, by the end of week two, I'd learned that he was English, and that he was in Boseman to earn his Master's degree in Environmental Engineering. I also knew that he had two sisters, one older, one younger, and that his arrogant façade hid an empathetic gentleman with a wry sense of humor.

None of that was comforting, and the little zing that went through me whenever we touched was even worse. To put it bluntly, it complicated my life. My boyfriend was nothing like Nick. On the plus side, Fred was a Montana boy, with a deep-seated love of the state's farm culture. We'd met the first week of freshman year when we'd bonded over both being from small towns and feeling lost in the city. He majored in animal sciences and planned to run an ecologically sound ranching operation—cattle first, and if he did well, expanding into horse breeding, as horses were his first love. His parents were pleasant and liked me as much as mine liked him. He had a stable future and was good to me and… And it sounded like I was writing a laundry list, not a love affair.

That's not fair, I told myself. I was just feeling distant because he'd had so little time for me recently. Never the best student, he'd been struggling with a couple of his courses, which took him away from me all too often. On top of that, he'd gone hunting or fishing every weekend this month instead of spending time with me. I was happy he had other friends, but a little less happy that our time together had lately consisted of apologetic texts and the occasional coffee-shop date between classes.

I'd just left one of those unsatisfactory meetings when I arrived at work Monday. Monday was my slow day for classes, so Fred and I should have had a good half-day to spend together. He had a morning Frisbee game, which he assured me wouldn't take long, but by the time he was ready to meet up, we had only a few hours before I had to be at work. The coffee date had deteriorated into a series of complaints, defensiveness, and eventually a strained silence only broken when I announced it was time for me to go to work.

Fred dutifully gave me a peck on the cheek and promised to make more time next week. I bit my tongue and excused myself. If I'd said what I thought, I probably wouldn't have a boyfriend at all. The thing was, I wanted him to have hobbies and friends and get good grades. I just wanted him to have time for me, too.

I welcomed the walking time from the coffee shop to the Wayward Wings to get my emotions under control and my head into work mode. During the walk, my phone dinged, and a message from my younger sister, Lizzie, appeared. I took a deep breath and opened the text. Lizzie's texts always distracted me. Being eleven was filled with excitement.

This time was no different. Lizzie wanted me to know that Bessie's pregnancy was coming along nicely, and that she'd found three abandoned raccoons and was hand-raising them.

I told her that Bessie, our one milk cow, was an old hand at calving and would surely have no trouble, and she needed to watch the raccoons carefully because they could learn to open cabinets and doors.

As usual, I felt better after the contact, even by text. Lizzie was a mini-me, a dreamy animal lover who adored books. Jenny, my other sister, was different. She also loved animals, but she was much more focused on their profitability than their cuteness. I expected she would do great things eventually—or at least be free of financial burdens.

Nick was already at work when I arrived. He'd picked up all the positions far quicker than I'd expected, and tonight he was working as bartender for the first time. It was the best-tipped position at the restaurant, and to be fair, Mr. McGregor allowed everyone who had mastered the job to rotate in the plum position. With that accent and smile, I knew Nick would rake in the tips, especially from the ladies.

Noticing that I had almost a half hour before I punched in, I stalked up to the bar and dropped my purse before slumping onto a stool. I couldn't help but smile as Nick's eyebrows arched, and he gave me a tiny nod. I imagined he was signaling, "You're next, Sweetie," but it was more likely he was thinking, "What are you doing at the bar instead of punching in and giving me a hand?"

By the time I finished my little daydream, the real thing materialized behind the bar in front of me and asked, "What can I get you, Em?

I smiled in spite of myself. He'd started calling me Em sometime toward the end of his first week, and I hadn't corrected him. Something about the way he said it, the look in his eyes… Or the fact that, although I didn't understand it, that look said he saw me in a different way than other people did.

"Hey, Barkeep," I said with a smile that was only partially forced. "I'll have a pop. Make it a double, would you? And throw in a king-sized plate of your best you-need-to-calm-down appetizer."

Nick kept a straight face. "Yes, Miss."

He turned away to fix my order, but I could see his shoulders shaking, as if he were trying to control his laughter. The dark cloud over me lightened.

Nick returned with a tall glass of cola and a colorful straw. "One pop, double, and the calming special of the day."

I nearly giggled at the way he said the word "pop." It was so cute in that accent.

With a flourish, he set down a plate in front of me. "Can I get you sauce to go with that?"

"I'm just not sure what kind I want," I teased.

Playing along, he shook his head with a grave look on his face. "I understand. Just a moment, Miss."

While he was gone, I stared at the plate. Nick must have been watching me over the past weeks, because all of my favorite appetizers were in front of me—fries, onion rings, and jerk wings. It was food heaven. By the time I had inventoried my feast, Nick was back with a tray of the appropriate sauces for every appetizer.

"Did I miss anything, Ma'am?" he said with a smug smile.

I picked up my pop and took a sip while I considered possible answers. The flavor smacked me in the face. This was no simple pop, unless you considered vodka pop.

I was quite sure my face had turned cherry red, and the grin on Nick's face confirmed it. He leaned across the bar, his large hands braced on the edge, and gave me a wink. "Don't worry, I put the cost of the drink in the register, so the till won't be off."

I knew I could handle one drink before work, and it wasn't like I had to drive anywhere or operate heavy machinery, so I took another sip. I normally never drank before work, but after fighting with Fred, I needed to take the edge off if I was going to make it through my shift.

"What's the big stressor today?" Nick asked casually as he dunked a glass in the sink behind the bar. "You usually take everything in stride."

"It's nothing really," I said, taking another sip of my drink. "I just had a little argument with… a friend."

Oh boy howdy. The moment I called Fred a friend, I knew I was in trouble. I wasn't sure why I hadn't mentioned to Nick that I had a boyfriend in the weeks we'd worked together, and now that we were fighting, it seemed like a bad time. I didn't want Nick to get a bad impression of Fred if I vented about him.

"It happens," Nick said with a sympathetic smile. "Everyone has a bad day now and then."

"I know, and for all I know, I could be the one who was out of sorts today. It was probably my fault."

"I can't answer that one," Nick said. "But you're pretty damn agreeable, from what I've seen."

Someone at the other end of the bar signaled to Nick, and he went to serve them. I thought about what he'd said.

I was a reasonable, laid back girl. Wanting to spend time with my boyfriend didn't mean I was demanding.

When Nick returned from the other customer, I finished the last onion ring and about half the drink and opened my purse. "Time to clock in."

Nick waved my money away. "That's on me, love."

Damn it, why was his accent so cute? I blamed the vodka.

"Thanks, but just this once. Next time, it's on me."

"Sure thing, Ma'am," he said, giving me a two-finger salute.

"That's right, Barkeep," I said with a grin. "And don't call me Ma'am. You make me feel like my mother."

He broke into a broad grin and called after me as I slid off the stool and headed for the timeclock, "Anything you say, Ma'am."

CHAPTER 3

The chilly wind was whipping my hair into knots as I walked the few blocks from my apartment to Wayward Wings, but I didn't mind. In fact, I was quite cozy inside my down jacket, jeans, and my favorite high-heeled boots. I only wore them occasionally because they didn't have enough traction for wet weather.

For once, I wasn't carrying half the MSU library with me. No classes today, and no work, either. Of course, I did have one textbook in my bag, but that was just in case Polly was late.

I was feeling surprisingly good in view of the fact that Fred was off playing Lacrosse this Saturday, then going out with the guys. Who needed him and his negative attitude, anyway? The crisp wind and gorgeous view of the mountains was enough for me.

Today I entered the Wayward Wings like most customers did, pausing as I walked in the door to scope out the best spot. Polly wasn't there yet, so I shrugged out of my coat, hung it on the half-empty coat rack, and walked over to my favorite barstool, all the way at the end of the bar. If she preferred, we could always move to a booth when she arrived or, because I was sitting at the end, facing down the length of the bar, she could sit on the long side, and we'd have our own little corner table. I liked dangling my feed off the high stools, which you couldn't do in a booth.

Nick was behind the bar, looking good enough to eat in a deep blue sweater that brought out the blue in his eyes, with a button-collar shirt underneath. He was not as overdressed for Boseman as he had been at first, but he was still the best-dressed man in the room. I covertly surveyed the male customers, then looked back at Nick.

I thought so.

Best looking, too.

He finished what he was doing and headed my way. "Well, well. What do we have here?" he smiled. "I didn't expect to see you today."

"I know. Pathetic, isn't it? Hanging around even though I'm not working."

For a moment Nick looked like he didn't know how to respond, so I let him off the hook. "Actually, I'm meeting my friend Polly here. She's usually late."

"I see," He actually looked relieved that I wasn't there alone. I wasn't sure why. "Want a drink while you wait?"

"Sure, I'll have…" I paused, trying to decide what I really wanted. Not a beer today, not a pop. Not the white wine women were drank so they wouldn't look like lushes or spill red on their clothes. I focused on Nick's waiting face. "I'll have a piña colada. Extra fruit on top please, and an umbrella."

He looked surprised, and I wondered if he'd ever made one. He didn't ask what was in it, though, so I didn't tell him.

While he was making my drink, I amused myself by watching him work. For a man who had never worked in a restaurant or bar before, he moved with amazing assurance, at least until he got to the umbrella part. I knew perfectly well we had no little umbrellas—the Wayward Wings wasn't a paper umbrella kind of place. He seemed to come to the same conclusion and substituted a little wooden skewer with three cherries and the rounded part of a cut lime on top. The effect vaguely resembled an umbrella.

He brought it over set it down, watching expectantly. I took a sip. It generally resembled a pina colada, maybe a little heavy on the pineapple. "Nice work," I confirmed, taking another small sip.

Nick looked bemused as I continued to take tiny sips, savoring the rare treat. "You do know it's only 3 o'clock, I hope."

"It's five o'clock somewhere." His blank look told me he wasn't a Jimmy Buffett fan. "It's part of an old country song," I explained.

"Ah," he said with a nod.

"You know, if you're going to be spending any time here in Montana, you're going to have to learn to love country music. Otherwise, you won't understand half the conversations you hear."

That made him laugh. I realized I'd only heard him laugh a couple of time, although he smiled often. I briefly wondered why, but my train of thought was cut off by Polly's arrival. She had her boyfriend, Adam, in tow.

I stifled a sigh. I would have preferred to have Polly all to myself, but I knew she didn't have much time with him. Although he was tall enough to be a basketball player, he was actually at MSU on a music scholarship and spent almost all of his free time practicing. A quiet boy, I always thought Polly liked him because he seemed content to indulge her endless talking without saying much himself.

Polly gave me a big hug, and after a bit of discussion, we decided to stay at the bar. Adam sat on the far side of Polly, who took her spot front and center, just the way she liked. Adam's seat allowed him to follow along with our conversation or tune it out and think about whatever he thought of when he was quiet. He could even talk to the guy a couple of stools down or Nick, if he chose.

Polly and I hadn't seen each other for a couple of weeks, although she was my best friend on campus. She had grown up on a ranch about ten miles from my parents' place outside Snowy Hollow, so we'd known each other since we were kids. Throughout grade school and into high school, we had ridden the same school bus. By the time I got on the bus, she always had all kinds of gossip about everyone on the bus before I could get a word in edgewise.

Nothing had changed. After asking me how I was, she didn't wait for an answer, but launched into an excited recap of everything she'd done and everything that happened since she last saw me.

Nick's appearance made her pause. She looked him up and down like a mountain lion ogling a nice haunch of venison, then ordered a light draft beer. Polly was always dieting, although as far as I could tell her weight never varied much. Adam ordered a non-alcoholic beer—he was afraid alcohol might interfere with his violin practice.

While Nick was getting their drinks, Polly leaned over and whispered accusingly, "You never told me about that!"

I grinned, feeling somewhat self-conscious for some reason. "I haven't seen you."

"You have a cell phone," she hissed. "You've been holding out on me."

I shrugged. "Maybe I wanted to surprise you. His name is Nick, and he's British. He's over here for some kind of post-graduate work. I got to train him."

That struck me as funny, since I'd resented Mr. McGregor making me do the training. However, I didn't try to explain to Polly why I was smiling. Too complicated.

"What else have you been up to that you haven't told me?" Polly asked, a look of mock suspicion on her face.

"Not much. I finally finished that team project, but Bella and I had to write Jim's section since he didn't do it. We weren't about to to fail because of one person, but we let the teacher know."

"That sucks. That's why I'm headed for law school. No group projects to deal with."

"I just don't think I could handle moving to a big city. I love the ranch too much."

"You could be a small-town lawyer and do wills and such." Polly smiled. We'd had this discussion many times before.

"I don't want to know all my neighbors' business and not be able to talk about any of it."

"That would be bad." Polly nodded, clearly trying to imagine how awful it would be to have all those secrets and not tell them. She was planning to work in corporate law, where the secrets she handled wouldn't be too juicy.

I glanced at my pina colada. Almost empty. One more wouldn't hurt, and all that pineapple juice would probably serve as dinner. I pushed my glass to the far edge of the bar.

"So what are you and Adam doing later? Going out to dinner?"

"We're going to grab hot dogs, then go to a recital at the School of Music. The question of the day is whether we go to Yeti Dogs or Paulie's."

"I'd take DQ over either of them," I said.

"So where's that boyfriend of yours?" Polly asked, a twinkle in her eye as she changed the subject.

"Playing Lacrosse, as usual." I didn't even try to hide my scowl. Polly knew all about my problems with Fred.

"You have a boyfriend?" Nick sounded surprised, and a little offended.

I looked up, surprised myself. I hadn't realized that he had drifted back to our end of the bar. I felt my face heat, though I wasn't sure why. "Yep," I said, nodding and trying to play off my own confusion.

"When did this start?" his voice was almost demanding.

I bristled. We were friendly, and maybe a few flirtatious moments had passed while we were on the go, bustling around the restaurant, but nothing that could be construed as anything other than innocent banter.

"Long before you wandered into Bozeman," I replied. "You sound surprised."

"I am." He was looking at me with the most bemused expression, as if I'd grown a horn in the middle of my forehead.

"Why? I may be a simple farm girl and not all... Suave or whatever, but I'm not a troll." I gave him a look. "Or maybe you think I am."

"Not at all." His denial was quick and sincere. "It's not that, Emily. I just... You never mentioned him." He turned to Polly and Adam. "Another round?"

After they confirmed that they wanted another drink, he scooped up my glass and left to make the drinks. I tried to regain my composure. Despite his denial, it still stung that he'd been so surprised that I had a boyfriend.

"What's that about?" Polly asked, cutting her gaze to Nick's back, where he was busy making my drink in the blender.

"Nothing," I said with a shrug.

"You didn't tell him about Fred?" she asked, raising her brows. "That's not like you, Em. Scandalous, in fact."

"Shut up," I muttered, trying not to blush at her teasing.

Nick wasn't done grilling me, either. Once he'd delivered our drinks, he leaned his lovely hands on the edge of the bar and looked at me sternly. "Is it serious?"

"Is what serious?" I shifted on the barstool, pretending ignorance.

"This boyfriend you've never mentioned." He frowned and added, "This boyfriend who's never come round to see you. Is it serious?"

He wasn't going to give up on this. I avoided his gaze and stirred my drink with the straw. "I'm not sure," I started. Then the grumbling spilled out. "I do know it gets less serious every time he chooses his Lacrosse team over spending time together."

"I've been telling her to dump him for months," Polly said. "He isn't right for her. Plus, if you ask me, he's just plain selfish. Who wouldn't want to spend time with you, Em? You're awesome."

"That's pretty harsh," said Adam. "Fred's not a bad guy. He's just a little immature."

"I swear," said Polly. "You would forgive a gray wolf from biting off your arm!"

"What if he was really, really hungry?" Adam said with a sheepish smile.

Polly shook her head with a grin. "What did I tell you?"

"Don't complain about being with the nicest man in this town," I scolded. Adam really was amazing. I couldn't imagine him harboring an unkind thought, and Polly was as lucky to have him as he was her.

"So this guy—this *Fred*—doesn't spend much time with you?" Nick asked, returning after serving another patron.

"He joined a Lacrosse team this year, and since then, we're like ships that pass in the night," I said with a dramatic sigh. "He's either studying, playing, or going out with the team… I mean, don't get me wrong, I'm happy for him. Everyone should have friends. But we haven't been on a real date since the semester started."

"That's dreadful," Nick said, looking genuinely concerned. "Did you go on those kinds of dates before?"

"The regular amount," I said, "Every week or two, we'd go to the movies, dinner…" I tried to remember what else we had enjoyed since we'd met. "Or go to the mountains for the day, do a little hiking, that kind of thing."

"You wouldn't have impressed me as a girl who likes hiking," he teased with a smile.

"You wouldn't have impressed me as a guy who likes working in a bar," I retorted, matching his light tone.

"One never knows. You might be surprised at what I like," Nick answered as he turned away to attend to another customer.

I wondered what that was supposed to mean for a moment before returning to how dissatisfied I was with Fred. If only I knew d no idea what to do about it.

CHAPTER 4

Monday morning came too early, but the phone alarm just wouldn't stop, so I struggled upright and brushed my hair back from my eyes. I grabbed the darn thing and gave it a swipe, and blessed silence flooded the room.

The silence gave me a moment to enjoy the morning as I looked out the window at a gorgeous late-fall day. The one tree I could see from the window had lost its leaves already, but the light pouring into the room promised good, if chilly, weather.

A hot shower got rid of the cobwebs, and I realized I was glad the week was starting. With the exception of drinks with Polly and Adam, it had been a lousy weekend. Not even a call from Fred, and homework from Sunday morning until I left for work. I'd tried not to be disappointed when I realized Nick wasn't scheduled until Tuesday, but I had been. He tended to cheer me up, and I had really needed some cheering up.

I didn't bother to check my messages until I had my oatmeal and yogurt ready. The first was a short message from Jenny, to let me know that Aurora, her bay mare, had foaled, and she'd named the colt Benji. It didn't seem like a really dignified name for an animal that could grow into a prize stallion, but I had to admit it was a cute name. I didn't raise my misgivings about the name in my congratulatory text.

There were also a couple of class reminders, a solicitation from my cell phone company, and a notice from my credit card company that I was approaching my credit limit.

The last text was from Fred. I braced myself before opening it. Every time we spoke, we seemed to argue. Oh well, get it over with.

I clicked to open the message and read it with surprise.

Emily, been kind of an ass. Dinner tnite?
Sure. What time?

By the time I'd washed the breakfast dishes, I had my answer:

Pick u up at 7

Since my last class finished at 5:30, that didn't give me too much time to get ready, but we both had early classes most days, so early dates were best. I wondered if he'd want to come over afterwards as I walked toward my first class. The idea gave me a funny feeling that I wasn't sure I cared for. I wasn't sure I really wanted him to come over, which made me feel guilty on top of everything else.

Shaking off my doubts, I reminded myself that nothing about Fred had changed since we started dating. I must be the one who had changed. Or maybe it was that Fred hadn't changed, hadn't grown emotionally since I met him.

I scolded myself for my unkind thoughts. I might not have had a date for Saturday night, but at least I had one for Monday. Fred was making time for me, which was all I wanted.

The day passed quickly, as most of my classes were fairly interesting. My long break in the middle of the day allowed me to get the morning's assignments done, so that wouldn't interfere with my time with Fred.

I kept checking my phone in case he texted me, hoping he'd tell me where we were going, but my phone was silent except for the usual robocalls. I could text him, but I was afraid he might consider it nagging. He was always accusing me of nagging him, although that's not the term I would have used. I just wanted to know what was happening.

It really didn't matter, though. Although Bozeman had a couple of fancy restaurants, he had never taken me anywhere that required more than a good pair of jeans or a casual dress.

My 4:30 class was not too complicated, so I did what I could to prepare for our date, trying to imagine scenarios that didn't end in a big fight or stony silence. It wasn't as easy as it should have been.

Imagining what I would wear was more productive. This relationship seemed to be teetering on the brink of something, so I decided to go all out, in a casual sort of way. By the time I got home about 5:45, I knew just what I wanted to wear.

A quick shower, hair up this time since I'd shampooed this morning, and a quick shave here and there, just in case... I blushed at the thought, which meant it had been way too long.

I started with my best red undies, the only set I had that actually matched. Then I pulled on a set of black tights—you didn't want to be flashing bare skin this late in November in Montana. Finally, I pulled on a sequined turquoise sweater dress with a moderately low neck, long sleeves, and a skirt so short I had to double-check to make sure nothing personal was showing from the back. I was pleased with what I saw in the mirror, but I wasn't done. Putting on a little fresh make-up, I added another layer of mascara to my lashes, and a touch more color than usual on my cheeks and lips.

I took my favorite necklace, a mountain lion carved of turquoise, and switched it from a chain to a black ribbon, which I tied around my neck to wear as a choker. Finally, I piled my wavy, auburn hair on top of my head, with long tendrils framing my face, and fastened a couple of turquoise clips in it. I added my favorite turquoise ring, a simple band carved with animal symbols, and considered applying nail polish.

Deciding that was too obvious, and also too much bother, I turned to my meager shoe collection. It was either the high black pumps or my favorite high-heeled boots, which were unfortunately brown rather than black. Still, the skirt was just too short for the pumps, and the brown boots gave a nice balance to the short skirt.

Finally, I went to the front coat closet and took out the only piece of clothing I really cared about. It was a three-quarter length beaver coat, with beautiful mink collar and cuffs. The coat had belonged to my grandmother and had been relined at least three times. Grandma had worn it until she died, and Mom had worn it until I was old enough. She paid to have it cleaned, the lining fixed, and have it stored each year. That was wonderful, but it also meant that there was a time when I would have to pass it down to Jenny, to enjoy until it was time to hand it on to Lizzie, my youngest sister. I just hoped to keep it until I married, in case I had a winter wedding.

For a moment, I tried to imagine walking down the aisle with Fred. I'd thought of it before, and although it didn't bring the rush of excitement people in movies and books always had, I'd always been a practical girl. Not everyone could have movie love, after all. Besides, maybe I just wasn't ready for marriage.

Why else would the image give me a distinct uneasy feeling?

I pushed the thought out of my mind and focused on where he might be taking me. Usually, we discussed these things, but he hadn't said a word. Did that mean it was going to be special? Trying not to get my hopes up too much, I considered the options. There was our favorite pizza parlor, where the wine was cheap and the pasta was hand-made; and the Montana Grill, whose bison was to die for. Maybe he'd even be feeling adventurous and take me out for sushi.

At ten till seven, I remembered that I hadn't worn perfume. I went to the bathroom and contemplated the three scents on the counter. One was a light, fresh scent that reminded me of flowers in an alpine meadow. I loved it, but it didn't match the outfit. Then there was my vintage scent,

Jungle Gardenia. I was crazy about it, but it made Fred sneeze. Lately, I'd only used it to put a drop in the bathtub when I treated myself to a hot bath.

That left the scent Fred had bought for my birthday. Piney with a hint of something bitter, I didn't care much for it. If the initial scent wasn't enough, the unpleasant undertone seemed to linger, and I could often smell it hours after putting it on. However, Fred had bought it, and every time I made myself wear it, he commented how much he liked it.

With a sigh, I applied it sparingly to my wrists and my navel, just in case. I just couldn't put it between my breasts or on my neck if I was going to be able to eat.

The doorbell rang as I was finishing up. I'd never given Fred a key or asked for one from him. When one of us stayed over, it was a one-night-at-a-time thing.

I didn't hurry to the door, because I wanted to look poised and gorgeous. I struck a deliberately casual pose as I opened the door.

"Dang, girl!" He gave a low wolf-whistle as he took in my outfit. "Aren't you dressed to kill!"

"Thank you," I said as I looked him over in return. Fred was always well-groomed, and tonight he looked exactly like he always did—plaid shirt hanging loose over comfortable jeans, with a down jacket on top of it all. At least it looked like he'd showered, as his hair was still damp.

Suddenly I felt awkward and overdressed, but I rejected that feeling. I wasn't overdressed, he was underdressed, and it was his fault, not mine, that he hadn't told me where we were going.

"Want a drink before we take off?" I asked, not sure if I wanted to change clothes.

"Sure, what you got?" He flopped down on the couch, leaving room for me beside him.

"Red, white, beer, rum."

"How about a rum and coke? We can save the wine for later."

At least I knew what his agenda for the evening was. I poured two rum and cokes, trying to shake my unwarranted irritation.

"So how's the lacrosse season going?" I asked, sitting down beside him with our drinks.

"Better than college," he said glumly. "I even hired a tutor, but I think I'm going to fail at least one class."

For a moment, my heart melted with sympathy, then I recalled that he'd used most of his study time, plus all of his girlfriend time, playing lacrosse.

I bit back a reply. I looked gorgeous, and I refused to act like a shrew, no matter how badly I wanted to. Fred brightened up almost immediately. "We're 5 and 3 on the field, though. If we win this season, MSU might add lacrosse to its sports roster."

"Really?"

"Yeah. That's what Tony says. He's the captain, he should know." He drained his glass. "How about one more before we go?"

I got up and poured another rum and coke, making it light this time. The last thing I needed was a drunken lacrosse player in my apartment. By the time we left, I knew that Fred's mother had been diagnosed with breast cancer, but her chances looked good, that his father had transferred to a job that didn't take him on the road so much. Fred was hoping for a new car for Christmas.

I had no idea why, since he already had a car. A lot of students lived near the University and walked or took the University bus to get around.

So far, he hadn't asked me anything about my life, except for his comments about my outfit. As he continued to pour out his troubles as if I was his confessor, not his girlfriend, I decided I was the one with the attitude problem. I smiled and nodded in sympathy. It wasn't like me to be so surly and out of sorts. I was happy we were spending time together, that he'd made time to hang out with me after not seeing him much this semester.

His glass was nearly empty, and he looked at me quizzically. I smiled and shook my head. "Actually, I'm really hungry. Let's go eat."

"You're right," he said. "Food first." He stood and headed for the door. When he shrugged into his jacket, I noticed that he didn't help me with my coat. He never had, and I'd never even noticed. I wasn't sure why I was being so nitpicky all of a sudden.

Once we were in the truck, I smiled at Fred, trying to lift my mood. "Why the new car?" I asked, patting the dash. "I like this one."

"Because I'm an only child," he said with a grin. "I get to have what I want."

I knew he was kidding, at least partly, so I grinned, my spirits lifting.

"You're gonna love where we're going," Fred promised.

"Where?"

"You'll see."

A minute later, he pulled into the Wayward Wings parking lot and shot me a broad grin. "I can't wait to see the looks on your customers' faces when you come in all dolled up. That really is a gorgeous dress, you know. Makes a man forget you're a little lean up top."

I stopped halfway out of the car to process what he'd just said. Lean up top? Although I was no Wendy Williams, he'd never complained before. Was this even the Fred I'd started dating? Or had I just always put up with his immature comments and laughed it off?

"Hey," I protested, trying to play it off as a joke even though his words stung. "My top is just as fabulous as the rest of me."

"Don't be like that," he said, throwing an arm around me. "You're great, but we all have strong points and weak points."

"Let's talk about something else," I said, slipping out from under his arm as we reached the wooden doors of the restaurant.

"Right," he said, seeming to realize that he'd crossed some kind of line, though he looked a little confused as to what I was upset about. I'd tried to hide it, but we'd been going out long enough for him to know when my smiles were forced.

"I made us a reservation," he offered, obviously trying to appease me. "Best seats in the house."

As we walked toward the door, Fred wrapped an arm around my shoulder and actually opened the door for me, something he never did. I wasn't sure if he was doing it for my benefit, or because he thought he was in the dog house with me, or because there were people watching.

We hung up our coats before Ayanna, the off-and-on hostess, led us to our "reserved" table. It was the only "reserved" sign in the whole restaurant, but there were plenty of empty tables, so it looked sort of silly, especially in a bar that served wings. But I appreciated the effort, so I offered Fred a smile and thanked him.

Nick appeared at our table, seemingly unaware that reservations were not a thing that usually happened here. Thank goodness for small favors. "Good evening," he said with a polite smile. "Would either of you fancy a drink to start you off?"

Fred raised a hand and pointed at me. "Rum and coke for both of us."

"Right away," Nick said smoothly, "But we do have a special tonight that I have to tell you about."

I drew my brows together. Old McGregor never did specials. He said that all of the food and drinks were special.

"Pina coladas are two-for-one," Nick said, giving me a little wink.

"Oh, I love pina coladas," I said, turning to Fred with an encouraging look. That was a little fancy for him, but I could sometimes convince him to branch out and get adventurous with me.

Fred looked confused, but he nodded. "I guess we'll have one of those, and just the rum and Coke for me."

"And shall I put in an appetizer for you? The lady knows the menu top to bottom," he said, with a conspiratorial look at me.

"I certainly do," I said with a smile. "Fred, how about the loaded fries and an order of onion rings? I'm starving."

Fred looked startled. I don't think I'd ever ordered two appetizers. However, I thought he might need to absorb some of the alcohol he'd been guzzling. In the past, Fred had drunk some, but no more than most college students. He seemed out of control tonight, and I couldn't help but wonder if he was more worried about his mom than he'd let on. We made it through the appetizers, and his second drink before he remembered to ask about how I'd been doing.

"What's been going on with you, Emily?" he asked, slurring his words just a little.

"Just working and going to school and checking in on my sisters," I said.

"Nothing else happening in your life?" he asked.

I was confused that he sounded a little belligerent.

"Nope, my boyfriend has been busy, so I'm pretty much just doing the usual. On the bright side, my grades are great this semester so far. No distractions." I winked to let him know I was kidding.

"That's not what I heard," he said, glowering at me.

Now I was really confused. "What did you hear?" I asked.

"I heard you were messing around with some other guy."

I was stunned, since I'd been working and studying and wondering why my boyfriend wasn't around. I tried to keep my cool, though. I had no idea what he was talking about, but the last thing I wanted was a huge scene in the middle of the dining room where I worked.

"What on earth?" I asked.

Before he could respond, Nick appeared, offering to freshen our drinks and bringing our main course.

I thought Fred was going to explode, but he de-escalated a bit as he accepted the Surf and Turf, a lobster tail with a 12-oz. ribeye. And ordered another drink—this time a double.

By this point, I'd lost my appetite and wanted nothing more than to make a run for the door. But I wasn't big on making scenes, so I took the food I'd ordered. The Wild Meatloaf was a fairly ordinary meatloaf except for the fact that they added a quarter pound of farmed buffalo to each pound of hamburger. It came plated with cooked greens, including a few dandelion greens, which they billed as Wild Prairie salad.

"You didn't want a steak?" Fred demanded. "It's your night Emily. You don't have to be cheap all the time. You could've gotten whatever you wanted out of me."

"I want meatloaf," I said, forcing a smile through the embarrassment. It was true that I was a little thrifty, since my family didn't have a lot of money, but Fred wasn't well-off, either.

"Does your new boyfriend get a bonus when you order the meatloaf?" Fred demanded, his voice rising as he glowered at Nick. "Where is that drink, *Bartender*?"

By now, I just wanted to duck under the table or go to the ladies' room and slip out the back door, but everyone was covertly watching. I straightened my spine and told myself to get through dinner and then it would be over.

I buttered two rolls and offered Fred one. "Did I tell you Jenny's mare foaled? She named the colt Aurora."

He slammed the bread I'd offered him down on the table, picked up the drink, and downed it in one long drink. "Don't try to change the subject, Emily. I know you've been fooling around with that new waiter! Everyone in town knows!"

I was sure they could hear him in the bar, which meant everyone in town would know by tomorrow.

"Everyone but me, I guess," I said in my most conciliatory tone. "Mr. McGregor assigned me to train him, that's all. There's nothing between us. Can't we just have a nice dinner? I've missed you."

"Yeah, right," he snapped. "You didn't show up for even one of my games."

"I have to work on Saturdays."

"I'll bet!" he sneered. "I bet it's real hard work spending all your time with that English prick."

I could hardly believe he, who was never available, was making accusations about me.

"I've had enough of this," I said quietly. "I'm leaving."

I stood to go, but he grabbed my arm. I tried to pull away, but he just held on harder.

"You're not going anywhere," he shouted. "Not sit down and eat your meatloaf!"

Seemingly out of nowhere, Nick appeared beside me and firmly peeled Fred's hand off my arm. "What seems to be the problem?" he asked, interposing his tall frame between Fred and me.

"You know what the damn problem is, you... you... " Fred trailed off as his alcohol-fogged brain searched for an appropriate expletive.

"I think the problem is that you've had a little too much to drink, sir." Nick's eyebrows drew together in what I'd learned to recognize as his stern look. "In fact, I've had several complaints. I'm afraid I'm going to have to ask you to leave. Would you like me to call you a cab?"

Fred made several false starts, but nothing came out except inarticulate, angry sounds. Finally, he pulled himself together. He slapped a few bills down on the counter and pulled his tipsy body up to his full height, though he was a good six inches shorter than Nick.

"You can have the cheating slut," he snarled. "Keep the tip. I'm glad to be rid of her."

Nick's fist balled at Fred's slur, but I grabbed his hand before he could deck him. Fred headed for the door, bumping into chairs as he headed for the door. As he took his coat from the coat rack, he threw my grandma's coat on the floor and ground his heel into it once or twice. Then he stumbled out the door.

I just stood there, trembling, tears pressing behind my eyes. All the dining room customers had witnessed my humiliation, and I wasn't about to add to it by crying in front of them.

"So sorry, love," Nick said, wrapping a strong arm around me and steering me to a quiet corner booth. He sat me with my back to the rest of the room, as if he knew I was about to lose it.

"Did he really leave?" I asked, my voice sounding pathetic even to my own ears.

"He's gone, Em," Nick said. "I'm sorry. Let me bring your food over here and check on my tables. No one can hear you here."

He slipped out of the booth and left me alone with his words. He must have seen I was on the verge of bawling my eyes out. I let a few silent tears slide down my cheeks before Nick delivered my food and gave me my space.

He took my plate away after I picked at my food, then delivered another drink and a coffee. "Are you all right?" he asked, his voice warm with concern.

"No," I answered honestly, "but I'm getting better by the minute."

"What was he going on about?" he asked.

My first instinct was to hide the embarrassing truth, but Nick was involved, like it or not. "I guess he thought I was seeing you on the side," I admitted.

"What ever gave him that idea?"

"I don't know. This is the first time I've seen him in two weeks."

"And he decided to end it by making a scene at your place of employment?"

"I guess so."

There was no way to make it sound better than it was, and it was truly awful.

Nick sat down in the booth beside me, his warm thigh pressing against mine. He slid his arm around my shoulders. "That wanker doesn't deserve you. You've never wavered from defending him since I came to Boseman. And I don't believe I've done anything untoward to make him think that."

All of that was true, and I nodded my head as more tears came.

He pulled me closer, and the safety I felt allowed me to shed a few more tears.

Then he dropped a bombshell.

"Of course, he's partially right. I'd never interfere in a relationship. But if you hadn't been in one, you're the only girl who's caught my eye since I've been here."

CHAPTER 5

After I'd eaten and called down, Nick cancelled moved me to my favorite spot—the lone barstool and the far end of the bar. He was supposed to be working the dining room, but after a discussion with Tiffany, who was tending bar that night, she headed for the dining room and he took over the bar. I knew Mr. McGregor wouldn't care, as long as the customers were served, but I wondered what he'd had to offer her to get her to switch places, since bartending was the plum assignment.

Of course, Monday bartending wasn't exactly something to fight about.

After he'd made sure that all the customers at the bar were served, he came over and leaned on the bar, his face just a few inches from mine. His blue eyes were dark with concern.

"You hanging in there, Em?"

"I'm just so embarrassed," I admitted. I could still feel the pink in my cheeks.

"Nothing to be embarrassed about. You weren't the one who made an ass of yourself," Nick said, reaching across the bar to pat my hand. "Besides, he'd have to be daft to think you'd cheat on him. I've known you for all of a month and I already know you're not the type."

"Thanks," I muttered. It was true. I had flaws like everyone, but I didn't have it in me to be duplicitous.

"Neither of us did anything wrong," Nick said firmly. "No need for embarrassment then."

"You're right…" I let my voice trail off, but I couldn't forget his last words in the dining room. I pushed the thought down.

"So here's what's going to happen," Nick said with his usual confidence as he straightened up. "You're going to have a nice drink, and when it slows down a bit, Tiffany and Elma are going to finish out the night while I walk you home."

"Oh, that's not necessary," I protested, even more embarrassed that everyone was being drawn into my stupid personal drama.

"Of course it is. We all agree that Fred was drunk and asinine. He could be waiting for you to cause another scene back at yours."

"All right," I agreed with a tentative smile. "I probably do need a companion to walk me home tonight. Thank you for offering."

While he worked the bar, pausing whenever there was a break to chat and offer moral support, I considered how I'd reacted to Fred dumping me.

Embarrassment—I hated being the centerpiece of an embarrassing scene.

Then, alarm. In all my life, that was the first time a man had put his hand on me in anger. My hand went to feel the spot where he'd grabbed me, and I found it sore to the touch. I'd probably have a bruise tomorrow.

Finally, anger. No one had the right to put their hands on me like that. The anger felt good, hot and expanding. And right. No one deserved what he'd done. If he'd do that in a public place, what would have happened if I had angered him when no one was around?

Okay, I was probably being dramatic. I knew Fred well. He'd had too much to drink, and he'd gotten out of control. I didn't think he was dangerous—but he was definitely a total jerk who had crossed the line.

Sitting at the bar, sipping on a chardonnay Nick had brought me, I searched my emotions to try and find heartbreak, sorrow, or even a little regret.

The only regret I could find was regret that I'd wasted a year and a half with such a clown. Beyond that, there was a tiny blossom of… hope? Relief? I wasn't sure, but it was more pleasant than any feelings I'd had for Fred in awhile.

On the short walk home, I let Nick slip his hand around my shoulder and help me balance on the ice that covered parts of the sidewalk. When we arrived at my apartment, we made sure Fred wasn't around. I didn't think he'd come to apologize or to start more trouble, and I was right this time. There was no sign of my now ex-boyfriend.

"Well, I guess I'm safe," I said, smiling up at Nick. "Thanks for walking me home."

"You're welcome, Em," Nick said with a gentle smile. "You've had a rough night. Get some sleep, and I'll see you tomorrow." He bent forward, and I closed my eyes, my heart exploding into a million butterflies as I froze, certain what came next. But his lips ended up on my forehead in a gentle, comforting kiss.

I relaxed and enjoyed the warm, comforting sensation, but a tiny part of me wilted wiht disappointment.

*

The next few weeks with Nick were a pleasant if confusing. We saw each other at least five days a week at the Wayward Wings, as McGregor continued putting us on almost the same schedule.

We worked beautifully together; lots of light banter, and what seemed like an almost telepathic connection that somehow made us aware of which customer needed something. Not that I believed in telepathy, but wasn't it odd that Nick might be tied up at the bar with a drunken patron, and I would suddenly feel the need to check on his martini girl at the other end of the bar? After the first few times, I wasn't even surprised when I followed a feeling and found a customer ready for a drink, some food, or their check.

Although he never mentioned it, the connection seemed to be two-way. If I was behind the bar, or waiting tables but occupied, somehow Nick managed to notice one of my neglected customers, and take care of them.

On the nights we weren't working together, Nick found reasons for us to spend some part of the day together.

One week it was the tree lighting Bozeman did each year, another it was a Christmas concert at the School of Music. Since Polly's boyfriend Adam was part of the show, it was only right that we be there to support him.

The concert was actually great, and sitting there with Polly on one side and Nick on the other, his arm casually around my shoulder, felt so right. Not sexy, not awkward, just *right*.

It was on that night, as we walked home through a light, feathery snow, that I mentioned the upcoming Christmas break, which was only two weeks away.

"I have to admit this has been a pretty rough semester. I'll be glad when it's over," I said, enjoying Nick's strong arm around my shoulders.

"It has been rough for you," Nick agreed. "What are you doing over the holiday?"

"Going home to the ranch. My sisters would kill me if I didn't show up," I said with a laugh.

"So it's a big occasion?" Nick asked.

"You have no idea. My mother is a little nuts where the holidays are concerned. Caroling with the neighbors a few days before Christmas, everything decorated to the point that it looks like Christmas threw up on the house, and all of the traditional foods."

"Just what are traditional American Christmas foods, anyway?"

I had to laugh. "I'm not sure if they are American traditional, but Mom's Christmas requires a Christmas goose, with some kind of odd stuffing no one touches but she insists on making every year, wild rice, green bean casserole, sweet potatoes, and whatever the girls and I cook up. Usually a pecan or mince pie. Jenny always insists on making macaroni and cheese, too, even though Mom has fits because it 'doesn't go' with the rest of the meal."

Nick burst into laughter and paused on the sidewalk. "That sounds delightful."

"Thank you for putting it so nicely," I said with a little laugh. "Basically, it's chaos with all of us in the house at once."

He nodded. "So what's in this stuffing you hate so much?"

"Some kind of dried fruit, bread, onions and celery, and a really weird tasting nut," I closed my eyes, trying to remember what else, since I never ate it.

"Let me guess. It has dried prunes and chestnuts."

"That sounds about right. Wait, don't tell me your mom makes the same abomination."

He sobered, turned me to face him, and somberly said, "I do believe your grandmother must have been English."

"She was, at least in part." I looked at him in confusion. "So what?"

"You just described half of a typical English Christmas menu. Just add some steamed pudding and perhaps Brussel sprouts..."

I turned and started walking toward my apartment. "Well, that explains why I didn't get ham or turkey like my friends," I said. "By the way, are you going home for Christmas?"

A shadow flitted across Nick's features. "Not this year. Mum and I are having a bit of a disagreement, and I've decided to be stubborn."

I was surprised. I'd done the usual sneaking around behind my mother's back when I was younger, even made up a few things over the years, but I'd never challenged her directly. Same with my dad, although he and I usually agreed, so it wasn't an issue. In fact, I suspected that he handled Mom very much like I did.

I would have loved to know what the conflict was, but he clearly valued his privacy. If he wanted me to know, he'd tell me.

"So," I asked, "What are you doing for the holidays?"

"I thought I'd volunteer at the Wayward Wings and give someone the time with their family."

"No way," I said firmly. "You can't do that. First of all, the Wayward Wings closes for Christmas Eve and Christmas Day. Too many students gone home to make it worthwhile. Second, my mother is already cooking, and she always makes way more than we can possibly eat. You can come to my house for Christmas!"

As soon as the words were out of my mouth, I realized how pushy I sounded. Nick looked uncomfortable, maybe even cornered, which only made it worse. Oh no. I'd overstepped.

I tried to lighten the suggestion with a joke. "Fusion is all the rage now, right? Who could pass up English-slash-American holiday fare?"

Nick cracked a smile. "Not me, I know that much."

"Oh good!" I said, unable to keep the happiness out of my voice. "Mom will love feeding a displaced Englishman. Besides, every foreigner needs to see a real ranch while they're in America."

"You live on a ranch?" he asked.

"Yep."

"I knew it," he said quietly. "Americans are all cowboys after all."

Now it was my turn to laugh. By the time we finished our arrangement, we were at the outer door of my apartment building. So far, I hadn't invited him up. I was on the third floor, and I reasoned that if he climbed two flights of stairs, he might feel entitled to more than I was willing to give.

"Thanks for walking me home," I said, fumbling for my keys.

"It's always my pleasure," he said.

Before I could find my keys, I felt his hand gently stroke the side of my neck. I raised my face to him, and he stepped forward. My heart leapt into my throat as his gaze dipped to my lips, and I knew what was coming. My lips parted, and he leaned down. His lips met mine, soft and sensual and comforting all at once. Tingles raced through my body like the snowflakes blowing across the parking lot—except these were warm instead of cold.

I wanted to pull him inside and drag him up to my room, but some voice inside my head warned me to take caution. Knowing my inner voice was correct, I made no move for the door, but I didn't pull away, either. I relaxed into his arms and, for once, stopped thinking.

When he finally pulled away, and my heart felt instantly bereft, abandoned.

He smiled down at me, stroking his thumb across my chin before planting one last, lingering but chaste kiss on my lips. His eyes were heated when they met mine, but he stepped back reluctantly. "I'll see you tomorrow, my sweet Em."

"Tomorrow," I whispered, trying to hold on to my balance, emotional and physical. I held on to the rail as I watched him walk away. By the time he was out of sight, I felt clear-headed enough to negotiate the two flights of steps to my apartment. Sometimes, I really hated being sensible.

CHAPTER 6

No matter how thrilled my parents were about my bringing Nick home for the holidays—they'd never liked Fred much—my feelings were much more complicated. I was less than a month out of a year-long relationship, one that had ended rather badly. And Nick was such a mystery. Even though we worked together most days, I knew so little about him.

He was English, his parents were both alive, and he had brothers and a sister back in England. He loved American hamburgers but detested peanut butter. He was hoping to go out and explore the countryside, especially the mountains, when spring arrived. He was a dynamite kisser.

Ah, yes. The kiss. The one, perfect kiss. The kiss he hadn't repeated, although he did seem more solicitous, more anxious to open the door for me, to take my elbow if the street looked icy, even to take the heavier tasks at work, which wasn't necessary but was very sweet.

I finished packing my bag, nervous at the thought of spending the next week at my house with Nick. He was so... Refined. I was... Not. I could get by when I was here, but at home, he'd see my whole family, and understand just how unrefined the Millers really were.

Outside of the separate garbage bag filled with presents, I needed very little. After all, I was going home. At least three quarters of my belongings were still there, including my really heavy winter wear, half of my clothes, and all the junk I'd collected since I was a little girl. My life was still there, even my old dog, Joe.

Joe was a mutt, but his mother had been a great cattle dog, and he was too. He'd always been my dog, and it had broken my heart to leave him behind, but at twelve years old, he really didn't need to learn about apartment living or be away from his beloved cattle. Sometimes when my family called, I'd have them put him by the phone, and he would bark and give his special little "miss you" sound, that other people thought was a growl. Lizzie had told me during our last phone call that he still went out when it was time to bring the cattle in, but lately he'd wait until they came into the home pasture to run after them, barking and nipping at their heels as if to prove he was still useful.

I dutifully did my mother's final walk-through of the apartment: balcony door locked, no water running, toaster, tv and computer all shut off and unplugged. Pulling my two bags out into the hallway, I locked the door, then hauled the bags down two flights of stairs and loaded them into the back of my old, reliable Blazer.

It was a ludicrous vehicle for an apartment dweller who walked everywhere, but its solid 4-wheel drive was perfect for the ranch life. And we had a tradition in our family. When Mom and Dad finished with a vehicle and bought a newer one, the reject car went to the eldest child who didn't have a vehicle. I'd drawn the Blazer when I was 16; Jenny had gotten some kind of Toyota, and Lizzie was still waiting for wheels.

I started toward the address Nick had given me. I tried not to wonder why he hadn't invited me over, or for that matter, invited me on a real date. He acted like he wanted more than friendship, but he hadn't pursued anything since our kiss.

I was surprised when I arrived at a gated community with a security guard who asked me who I was there to see. I'd never been to Nick's but some part of me had assumed he was an exchange student and lived on campus. When he'd given me his address, I had just assumed he lived in one of the apartment complexes that were popular with students. Not... This.

"Just a moment, Miss," the guard said after I'd told him I was there to see Nick Lancaster. Stepping away, he held his phone to his ear, presumably calling Nick to check my credentials. It seemed like an eternity before he turned back to me, smiled, and nodded, hitting the button to lift the gate.

"Straight ahead, and right on the third street. He's on the left, Miss."

"Thank you."

I'd known that we had a couple of gated communities in Bozeman, but I'd never expected that Nick, or any MSU students, to live in them. Especially not someone who needed a job at Wayward Wings. Our tips sure as heck didn't pay for this.

I'd sort of reconciled my image of Nick with the gated community by the time I pulled up in his driveway. He was suave and gentlemanly, after all. His house was a large, two-story home. What MSU student could afford a house like that? Maybe he had a bunch of roommates. No, I couldn't imagine the homeowners' association approving something like that. Did he have a family he hadn't told me about? How old was this guy, anyway, and what did I really know about him?

I wasn't about to walk up to his door and knock, so I texted him that I was outside. Nick appeared promptly with two large, overstuffed bags. He waved at me before disappearing back into the house. This time, he came out with two more pieces of oddly shaped luggage.

I wasn't sure, but it looked like he stopped and talked with an unseen person right inside the doorway. For all I knew, he had a wife and kids!

No, that couldn't be. He wouldn't be leaving them to spend Christmas on a ranch with strangers. Maybe he was just keying in a security code.

"Do we have enough room for all this?" he asked as he got to the car with the four overstuffed bags.

"Sure, it's a Blazer. We can fit anything into it," I replied, opening the back of the vehicle. "Are you planning on moving in with my parents, or did you pack three outfits for each day?"

Nick blushed a little. "Of course not. It would be rude to show up without gifts for your family, since they're taking me in for so long. And I wanted to bring a little touch of England to the celebration, so I ordered a few things from home and talked Tommy into cooking up a real Christmas pudding."

"You didn't have to do all that," I said with a smile. "My family is just happy I'm not bringing Fred home for Christmas."

"Not as happy as I am." His blue eyes sparkled.

As we both climbed into the front of the Blazer, I asked, "So, who's Tommy?"

"He's my…" Nick paused a long moment before continuing. "My manservant."

Now, I was really confused. "Manservant?"

"Butler. Housekeeper. Occasional cook. I don't know the American word for it."

Rich, I thought. The American word for having hired help was rich, which my family most definitely was not. My heart sank. If he was accustomed to that style of living, he was going to be in for a big disappointment at my house. I had no idea how to respond, or even how to think about someone who had their own personal servant, so I concentrated on driving.

"He's flying home for Christmas," Nick explained. "Don't worry, he won't be alone for the holidays if I go to yours."

I tried to brush away the thoughts of what a big mistake I was making by bringing him to my family's ranch. He would have been alone otherwise, so maybe he wouldn't judge me too harshly for being an ordinary American. "I need to gas up before we leave town for the drive," I said briskly. "Want to pump the gas or get the snacks?"

It took him a second to answer, and I would swear that he was doing some kind of internal calculation. "I'll pump. Regular or premium?"

"Regular," I said with a smile. "What kind of snacks do you like?"

"Something American." He grinned. "I'm a tourist, after all."

As I headed into the store, I did the math. He was paying for gas, bringing food, and delivering presents. He had to like me, otherwise why go to so much trouble to impress my family? Or was he just so rich that he did this with everyone he knew?

Having no idea what kind of snacks he would want for the drive out to the ranch, I got all my favorites, as well as each of my sisters' favorites—Flamin' Hot Cheetos, Gas Station Pizza, Pringles, Christmas tree-shaped chocolate-covered marshmallows, and hot chocolate to keep us cozy on the drive. I scurried across the parking lot, the icy wind whipping tiny snowflakes against my cheeks. When I was at the car, arranging the snacks as best I could around the middle console, Nick leaned in from where he was getting gas.

"Now that's a feast," he said. "Probably what I would have been eating for Christmas dinner had I not gotten such a generous invite."

I straightened up and started around the Blazer to get in the driver's side, but before I could, I stopped dead in my tracks at the sight of a family figure. What were the chances, and why, oh why, hadn't I picked some other gas station?

I stopped at the open driver's side door when Fred waved at me from the next pump, where he was filling up. He had a blonde in the passenger's seat of his truck. He stepped away from it to sneer at me. "I see you've replaced me quick enough."

I couldn't help myself.

"Wasn't hard to replace you." I wanted to stop, but I just couldn't help myself. "There was a line hoping I'd see you for what you are."

That was a lie, and it didn't make me feel better the way I thought it would.

"And you picked the rich guy," Fred said, shaking his head. "Predictable."

"I picked the gentleman." The words were out of my mouth before I registered what I'd said, but at least these ones were true.

Fred's lips pulled back in an obnoxious sneer. "Well, I hope it works out for you. Matches between farmers and royalty rarely work."

I couldn't help myself, although his remarks tore at me. Fred had more money than me, but that wasn't why we'd dated, and it certainly wasn't what drew me to Nick.

"What about matches between jerks and Barbie dolls?" I snapped. I turned and climbed into the Blazer. It's possible that he was shouting something obscene as I closed the door, but I couldn't hear the exact words and really didn't care. I knew it was kind of petty, but it felt good to have gotten the last word.

I wanted to gun the engine as I drove off, but I refrained out of propriety. Nick and I were both quiet as I guided the Blazer onto Highway 84. It wasn't a superhighway, but it took us home through Norris, where my friend Shelby had settled with her husband and ran a mostly-online candy business. I'd alerted her that I was coming, and she had a fairly huge order of real chocolate cherries, fudge, walnut divinity, and a big box of mixed candied nuts and chocolates ready for me.

"Thank you," Nick said, sounding a bit tentative.

"For what?" I asked, surprised.

"For telling what's-his-name that you preferred me."

I felt my cheeks reddening. "About that... I realize I overstepped. I was just so mad, I didn't want him to think I was some loser who couldn't get a boyfriend. Sorry. I didn't mean to imply..." I stopped, at a loss for words, because that's exactly what I'd meant to imply. That was the whole point in saying it.

"Oh, then we aren't?" he asked.

"No." My face burned hotter. "I mean, are we? After that kiss, I thought maybe... But then nothing else ever happened."

Nick sighed. "So did I. I mean, I thought that, too. But it's complicated."

"What's so complicated? Because you're English? People from different countries get together all the time."

"That's true, but... It's more complicated than that."

"Because your family won't like me," I said, the realization dawning. He was rich as a king. I was a farm girl. Just like Fred said, it would never work out. Besides, if it lasted, would either of us be willing to move to another country entirely?

"Of course they would," Nick protested. "This is my fault. Do you want me to beg off from spending the holiday with your family?"

That brought me back to earth. "No, of course not. Whatever happens with this spark we... *I*...feel, we're friends, and friends don't let friends spend Christmas alone."

"We both feel it," he reassured me. "If I was holding back, it was only out of respect for you, Emily. I think very highly of you."

It wasn't exactly a profession of love, but I knew Nick wasn't the most emotionally demonstrative, so I let it be.

Before too long, we arrived at Norris, barely more than a wide spot in the road, but with its own small claim to fame:

Norris Hot Springs. Shelby and her husband had found a beautiful cottage with a front room that was just made to sell candies from, almost across from the hot springs and campground. From there, she sold a few candies to campers and ran a robust online candy business.

Although we texted every week, Shelby and I had a lot to catch up on. Her husband Jordan worked on his parents' ranch a few miles out of town, and he was gone for the day, so we chatted it up for a few minutes while I picked up my order. Shelby raved about her wonderful life with Jordan and how good her business was doing. Jordan was such good husband material—attentive, talkative, and a hard worker to boot. Compared to Fred, he was the perfect husband. For Shelby, not for me. Jordan and I had gone out on a couple of dates in high school and decided by the second date that we were better as friends. I'd introduced him to Shelby, thinking they might hit it off, and the rest was history.

Once we were back in the Blazer, heading for my home, I grinned at Nick. "So, what do you think of rural Montana?" I asked.

"Breathtaking," he answered.

We turned onto Highway 287 and cruised through McAllister before coming to Ennis, where we turned. We'd end up in Twin Bridges, just a short drive to the ranch. When we finally got to the dirt road, Nick leaned forward and peered out the windshield. "Are you sure this is the right way?"

I couldn't help but laugh. "It's the right way."

"I've been dying to get out into the wilderness since I got here," he said. "What an unexpected surprise."

"Well, this isn't exactly wilderness, but it's more wild than Bozeman," I admitted. "And probably much more wild than most of England."

He grinned. "You have no idea."

Sometime during our conversation, he had taken possession of my right hand, which kind of felt like having a secret path to heaven.

We fell into a companionable silence, which was interrupted by a bang, followed by a few bumps as I put on the brakes. Damn. A flat tire.

Nick and I climbed out of the car and stared at the driver's front tire. Completely flat, which meant something must have punctured it. With the temperature hovering in the single digits, it was not my favorite time for changing tires.

"Oh, good grief," Nick said, looking positively stricken.

"Damn. I wanted to get home clean and cute," I said with a sigh. "Not today."

I headed for the back of the Blazer, opened it up, and began moving suitcases. Nick joined me immediately. "What do we do now?" he asked.

That seemed like such a strange question to me that I straightened up from rearranging the luggage. "What do you mean?"

"I don't know." This time he sounded a bit defensive. "Call someone to fetch us?"

I couldn't help but laugh as I shook my head. It was impossible to even imagine a towing company servicing this gravel road, and I couldn't just leave my car here. "No, silly," I said, swatting Nick's arm. "We change the tire."

CHAPTER 7

I couldn't help but laugh at Nick's dubious expression when he realized I meant to change the tire myself.

"It's not that big a deal," I assured him. "Easy peasy. My dad insists I keep a real spare in the car, not one of those little donuts, and he taught me how to do this when I was ten years old. Living on dirt, you gotta know how to change a tire."

Nick didn't seem to have any idea about the whole process, so I finished moving the suitcases and uncovered the spare tire. When I started to unscrew the screw that held it in place, he took over with that, so I dug out the jack and assembled it.

"What's that contraption?" he asked, examining it suspiciously.

"This is the jack," I said. "It lifts the car so you can get the flat off." I demonstrated, and he nodded.

"Do you think I could give it a go?" he asked when I crouched to slide the jack under the car. "Might come in handy some day. You never know."

"Sure," I said, nodding. "I'll walk you through it."

"You're a gem," he said, taking over when I moved aside. Although he had clearly never changed a tire, he worked at it valiantly, and I let him follow my instructions, even though I could have done the work far more quickly. I was thankful to keep my fingers warm in my pockets, and he seemed determined to finish the job.

He had a few smudges of tire dirt on his expensive sweater when we finished, but he didn't seem to notice. He beamed proudly as he stood from the successful operation.

"What do we do with the old tire?" he asked, his brow furrowing in concern.

"We toss it in the back and take it with us," I said, gesturing with my thumb. "Dad will put a plug in the hole, and it'll be good as new."

Nick looked startled. I guess he'd never thought of re-using an item after it broke. That was rich folks for you.

Once we were back in the car and on the way, Nick asked, "How much farther to your parents farm?"

"About an hour and a half," I replied. "There's a shorter route, but with the stops, this is the best way overall."

"I don't mind the drive." He scooted the seat back to make more room for his long legs and stared out the window. "This is lovely. I can see why you never left Montana."

I couldn't help glowing a bit, as if I was responsible for the wild landscape. "Thanks."

"We don't have anything like this in England or even on the continent."

Obviously his family had enough money to travel some. "But England is so green," I protested. "And there are amazing mountains in Europe—the Alps, the Basque country…"

"Those are indeed beautiful, but for the most part, they're not that wild. All this open space is…" His voice trailed off. "I really don't have the words to express it."

We didn't talk much until we reached Sheridan, but at some point, Nick's hand ended up resting comfortably on the back of my neck. I said nothing for fear he would move it.

The stop in Snowy Hollow was shorter than the Norris visit. I'd been saving since last Christmas and had ordered some leather goods for all of the family—a jacket for Mom, new gloves for Dad, and matching hats for the girls. It was only recently that I had made an addition to my order: a rawhide vest for Nick. Sizes could be hard to judge, but he was obviously a x-large shirt, and a vest could be adjusted. Because I couldn't help myself, I had asked Evan to do some leather fringe on the vest. It was a little expensive for a "might be" boyfriend, but I figured the look on Nick's face when he opened it would be worth the expense.

Nick seemed fascinated by Evan's leatherwork and asked dozens of questions as Evan showed him around the workshop. I concentrated on getting the gifts into the car without letting Nick see his present. Afterwards, we drove through the cozy little town with lights twinkling on the gazebo in the square and a big tree. I loved our town, the closest one to the ranch, even though we lived a ways out. As a teenager, I'd spent evenings caroling, helping decorate, and handing out canned goods in the weeks leading up to the holidays, and I missed it now that I was away at school.

The rest of the trip to the farm was pleasantly uneventful. Nick alternated between holding my free hand and resting his arm on the seat so he could rest a hand on my shoulder. I pointed out interesting sights and talked about the area's history. His questions told me he was truly interested, and when we drove by a herd of antelopes grazing with some cattle, nothing would do except to stop so he could get pictures. He would've passed out from excitement if I found some elk for him, or even better, a mountain lion.

I always loved arriving at the ranch. Set in a valley with hills and mountains rising behind it, that first moment, when I came over the hill and saw it all spread out below, green in spring, golden in fall, or white in winter, it always took my breath away. I pulled to a stop at the top of the hill, spread my arms to take in the scene, and said "Here it is. Rochester Creek Ranch."

"Oh, how lovely," Nick exclaimed. "You didn't tell me you were raised in the middle of paradise."

I chuckled. "I didn't really appreciate it until I went to Bozeman for college. It always seemed exciting, visiting the 'big city.' But living there really isn't my thing."

He smiled wistfully at me. "I can't imagine you living in London, dealing with real congestion and crowding."

Maybe he was thinking how impossible a future with me was, too. I pushed the thought away and focused on the excitement of the holidays. "Here we go," I said. "I have to warn you. My family is a bit nuts. Jenny and Lizzie are completely excitable, and Dad's not much better."

I had to smile as I thought of Dad. "When I was eleven, I wanted my own horse for Christmas. Dad told me it just wasn't the time, that I was too young to take care of a horse, that winter was the wrong time to start a new animal on the farm, that he couldn't afford it, so I shouldn't get my hopes up. I had learned not to trust Dad about these things, so I suggested that Santa might bring me a horse, 'preferably a palamino, at least 16 hands, as I planned to grow some more.' He guffawed and told me I was too old to believe in

Santa, and maybe I should start looking for an after-school job to buy my horse."

I paused, smiling at the memory.

"Then what happened?" Nick demanded.

That brought me back to reality. "On Christmas morning, I went down to breakfast and Dad wasn't there. When I asked where he was, Mom turned away. Jenny announced, "We don't know. He went out after you went to bed, looking for Dora and Isabel. He hasn't come back." Her eyes were wide, and she looked absolutely terrified, so I never questioned it. Remember, I was eleven."

"Go on then."

"By the way, Dora and Isabel were two yearling heifers who shouldn't have been out in the pasture by the barn."

"Then what?" Nick urged, clearly as engaged in listening to my story as I was to telling it.

"Jenny said he'd forgotten his phone, which was on the counter. That should have clued me in, but I was in a panic by this point. 'Did he say which way he was going?' I demanded. My sister said he was checking the meadow halfway up the hill, where he'd found them before. By this time, I was totally in a panic. I jumped up from the breakfast table and started putting on my heaviest winter gear, even though it was around 30 degrees. I said I'd go get him, and they should all stay there, in case he showed up."

"At this point, Mom chimed in. 'You shouldn't do this Emily. It's dangerous out there. Your dad is a grown man.' I heard her say something under her breath. Later, I figured out she was muttering 'at least he's supposed to be.' But I just had to do it. I took Dad's phone, so they could call me in case he came back.

"There was about a foot of snow on the ground, but it wasn't all that cold. In the barn, old Neddy was enjoying a late breakfast of yummy grain, with just the right touch of molasses. He was still sound and perfectly able to carry a rider, but not inclined to do so without some persuasion. He glared at me as I saddled him up, but seemed to sigh his acquiesce when I gave him a crispy fall apple and promised more if he found Daddy.

"Up the hill we went, the snow spraying out behind us with every step. Neddy wasn't inclined to move fast, either, no matter how often I kicked him in the ribs with my snow boots. One step at a time, we moved up the snowy hill.

"You've probably guessed it already, but when we *finally* got to the meadow, Dad was there with Dora and Isabel on a rope lead. He was riding Zeus, his coal-black gelding, and beside him, wearing a tooled-leather saddle and harness, was the most beautiful horse I'd ever seen. Pale gold with a snowy mane and tail, she was dancing in the snow, obviously bored and ready for something to happen.

"My first feeling was a huge wave of relief. Dad was alive and well. Then came fury. He'd nearly scared me to death. Finally, joy, excitement, and love. I told him he'd nearly scared me to death, and he said that was the whole idea. He asked what I was going to name her. I already had one picked out—Iris, the goddess of rainbows."

"Well, you were only eleven," Nick said, arching a brow at me.

"Hey," I protested with a laugh. "That's a very good name, I'll have you know. I jumped down from dirt-brown Neddy, gave him a reward apple, a good nose scratch, a little nose kiss, and handed his reins to Dad."

I still recalled the first time I approached Iris. Very slowly, I moved toward her, as she danced on coltish hoofs in the snow. She calmed a little when I held out my hand, with a nice carrot in it, and nibbled it delicately. Reaching up to rub her mane, I reached into another jacket pocket and pulled out an apple, and the bond was made. I could feel it as clearly as if it had been a steel chain connecting us. I looked deep into her golden-brown eyes, and she looked back, even before chomping the apple. Our bond was sealed, a love that would last for both of our lives.

Placing a foot in the stirrup, I swung up into the saddle that felt like it was made for me. I held the reins loosely, and whispered, "Iris. Beautiful Iris."

By the time we made it back to the ranch, I'd forgiven Dad and my siblings for their deception. I'd also fallen in love with Iris, and by the time I had rubbed her down and given her an extra portion of molasses-rich grain for her efforts, I was hers, and she was mine.

I finished telling Nick the story as we headed down the dirt road that led to the ranch. Pulling to a stop in front of the house, a sprawling ranch house that faced the mountains,

I turned to him, butterflies in my belly. "Here we are. Watch out for my sisters, they're a menace."

"I'll keep that in mind," Nick replied, laughter in his voice.

CHAPTER 8

The minute the car came to a stop, we were surrounded by my family. Mom headed straight for my door, pulled me out and nearly smothered me with a hug. Dad stood back just a bit, waiting his turn until I wrapped him in a bear hug. As to Nick, he barely had a chance to get out of the car before my sisters made a dash for him. Watching from one eye as I hugged Dad, I noticed that they weren't jumping all over him. Instead, they were executing perfect English curtsies. I guess they had figured out that he was English.

Nick's face took on a grave expression as he solemnly bowed in response to their curtsies.

Jenny looked down and said, " Jennifer Miller at your service, sir."

Nick's lips curled into an amused smile. "Charmed, Ms. Miller," he murmured, repeating the ritual with Lizzie, who for this occasion had become Elizabeth.

I hardly had a chance to be embarrassed at my sister's behavior before my father stepped over to Nick and held out his hand. "John Miller. Happy to have you with us for the holidays."

Nick grasped his hand firmly and gave him a robust handshake, the kind Dad liked. "Nick Lancaster, sir. I appreciate the invitation. It means the world to me to have someplace to spend Christmas, since I'm here in the states by myself."

"We're real happy to see you here with Emily, too," Dad said. "Can't say much for that fellow she was seeing before."

"I probably shouldn't say this," Nick said, dropping his voice as if I couldn't hear, but flashing a conspiratorial smile at me. "But I couldn't agree with you more."

My father chuckled. "Good man. I'd love to stay and chat, but I have a little problem in the barn. You know anything about cows?"

"Only that they are ruminants and that they produce milk," Nick said with a broad grin.

"You want to learn a little more?" Dad asked with a glint of humor in his eye. "I've got one about to calve."

I cringed. It was just like Dad to take one look at a city guy and decide to have a little fun with him. It would probably scar poor Nick for life.

"That's okay, Dad," I said quickly. "We've got to get these bags inside."

"Just leave 'em," Dad said. "It'll only take a minute."

"Please don't," I begged. "He's already had to help me change a tire."

"Don't touch the bags," Nick said, grabbing my hand and giving it a quick squeeze. "I insist. I'll bring them in just as soon as I've visited with your father. Okay?"

"You didn't know how to change a tire?" Dad asked in disbelief.

"I do now, thanks to your brilliant daughter," Nick said. "I'd love to learn about the cattle as well."

"You really wouldn't," I told him with a grimace. "It's not pretty."

"Nonsense," Nick said. "I want to know all about your life, Em. I'll be back in no time."

As they headed for the barn, I pressed my eyes tight shut and resisted the urge to throttle Dad or cling onto Nick and beg him not to do it. He had no idea what he was getting himself into.

My dad was a legendary practical joker, though, and he couldn't resist the urge to prove that ranching was as tough a job as any wealthy man had.

I turned to Mom, trying to distract myself from what was surely a frightful scene for poor Nick. "Which one of the cows is calving, Mom?"

"It's Bessie," she said. "You know how she can be."

Bessie was one of only two milk cows on the ranch, all the rest were beef cows, kept for sale. Two cows produced far more milk than our family needed, but with only one, there was always a gap in milk production. We used the rest to feed the pigs, who loved it, and to make cream and butter. Of the two milk cows, Bessie was a special pet, having come to the ranch when I was only five. She was also temperamental, especially when she was expecting, but she loved all of us in her bovine way.

Mom seemed calm as always, but when I turned to my sisters, I was dismayed at the worried look on their faces. "What's wrong?" I asked.

Jenny burst into giggles and hid her face in her mittens.

As the men walked off and my mother retreated to the kitchen, I turned in either direction, not sure what to do. Surely Dad wouldn't do anything awful, like asking Nick to help pull a calf. I simply couldn't picture Nick elbow deep in old Bessie's business. Dad wouldn't do that, would he? I thought I might actually die if he did.

Before I could worry more, Lizzie grabbed me by the hand and all but dragged me toward the front porch. Jenny headed the other way.

We all arrived at the glassed-in back porch about the same time, Lizzie with me in tow, and Jenny with a tray of cups of cocoa and Mom's famous Christmas cookies.

"You made the cookies without me?" I asked, feeling left out, even though I couldn't expect them to wait for me when I hadn't come home until Christmas Eve day.

"You weren't here," Jenny pointed out. "We can make more."

"True," I said, a warm feeling filling me up at the familiar crunch. Jenny handed out steaming cups of hot cocoa, and I snuggled back on the sofa.

I choked on the first sip from the mug, though. My cup was half full of Kahlua, which I certainly needed by this point, but which my little sisters had no business drinking.

"Don't worry," Jenny said as she held out her cup. "There's none in ours."

"There better not be." I scowled at my two little sisters. "Now what on earth is going on?"

The girls dissolved in giggles. "Do you think she really doesn't know?" Lizzie gasped, as soon as she could stop laughing.

"Know what?" I demanded.

"I don't think she does," Jenny said and dissolved into laughter. "She's gonna need that drink!"

"What is wrong with the two of you?" I asked in frustration. "Have you lost your minds?"

"How did you meet Nick?" Lizzie asked, sobering and wiping away a tear of laughter.

"He works at Wayward Wings with me," I said. "I trained him."

"And?"

"And he's English, and he's going to MSU. We've been getting to know each other pretty well, I think. He really loves the mountains."

"What about his family?" Lizzie pressed.

"They live in London, from what I gather. He seems to get along with them fine, but he didn't go home for Christmas this year, so I brought him here." Her questions were making me realize how little I really knew about his background. Mostly I knew how his eyes lit up when he looked at me, how being close to him made me feel.

Jenny snorted. "You didn't think to ask why he wasn't going home for the holidays?"

"I did," I said, sitting up and raising my chin. "He had a fight with his mom."

"And you haven't picked up a *People* magazine in this century?" Lizzie demanded.

"You know I don't have time for celebrity gossip. What does that have to do with anything?"

Jenny giggled again. "You tell her," she said to her sister.

"You really don't know who you're dating?" Lizzie asked, her eyes wide. "Doesn't the name Lancaster mean anything to you?"

"Is there something it should mean?"

"You do know England has a Queen, don't you?"

By now my frustration was about to boil over. "Lizzie, stop playing games. The queen is not a Lancaster. What does she have to do with this?"

"The Queen has no last name, and technically, neither do her sons…"

I stared at my sister, a hollow sense of dread beginning to grow in my stomach. "Yes, so?"

Lizzie stared at me as if I were daft. "So, they probably take the last name of the nearest relative if they're required to do something like, I don't know, apply for college."

"There have to be hundreds of Lancasters in England. Maybe thousands," I protested.

"Yes, but only one Nicholas Lancaster who made the front page of my favorite magazine this summer. There was a big stir when he decided to transfer to a U.S. university."

"That's impossible. He's working at the bar with me." I suddenly felt adrift, and it wasn't a good feeling. "Why would someone who's a relative of royalty be working at a bar?"

"Not a relative of royalty," Jenny corrected, ignoring my question. "He *is* Royalty. To be exact, he's a prince. *The prince.*"

"That's impossible," I said weakly. "He'd have a... A bodyguard or something."

"Why do you look so upset?" Lizzie asked. "You just brought home Nicholas Lancaster, the Quiet Prince. His brother is flashy and makes the tabloids more, but Nick is first in line for the Throne, and sure to get there, if you figure out the relative ages of the other two possibilities. And the two of you seem pretty friendly, which means we could all soon be *royalty!*"

My head was spinning. Jenny seemed so proud, but I couldn't muster the same excitement. Instead, I felt stupid, naive, and somehow betrayed. Why hadn't he told me? He'd never given even a hint. And that wasn't some small thing to lie about, like eating someone's awful cooking and saying it was delicious just to spare their feelings.

Before seeing his house, I'd guessed he wasn't going home for Christmas because money was tight. After all, wait staff didn't make that much at a place like ours, and transatlantic flights were costly.

But obviously that wasn't the case. The best explanation I could come up with was that I was just a diversion, someone to occupy his time while he finished up his education, company until he went home to his privileged life and his royal friends. That was better than thinking he'd been laughing at me behind my back all this time because I hadn't realized who he was. I just didn't pay much attention to famous people, especially ones from other countries. Maybe if he'd told me he was the Duke of Whatever, I'd have realized it from the start. But he'd introduced himself like he was any other commoner.

That's what royal people called us, right?

All I could think was that I needed to get away—away from my teasing sisters, away from the fact that my budding dreams of love had just come crashing down, away from Nick.

I jumped up, made an excuse, and hastily left the porch. I needed some time alone to sort out my thoughts, without my sisters or my mother or father.

As for Nick... Nick!

He'd left with my dad to go tend to Bessie. I swayed on my feet. If my dad had convinced the prince of England to stick his arm up Bessie's butt, I would just die! I took off for the barn at a dead run, hoping against hope that my father hadn't done anything to embarrass me too badly in the eyes of the prince.

The barn was down the hill from the house, and I was a little out of breath by the time I got there. I couldn't think of anything but the unfolding disaster.

Nick was just coming out of the barn, looking a little shell-shocked and grinning like a fool. My father was a few steps behind him.

"Your boy here just helped with the birth of a beautiful little Jersey heifer," Dad boasted. "I don't think he's got a medical career any time in his future, but he didn't faint dead away, which is more than I expected, if I'm honest."

I fixed him with a glare that could drop the temperature of a Montana winter, and he edged away.

Nick was busy filling me in. "Emily, that was amazing! I helped bring a life into the world. I even helped dry her off. Can you imagine? Me, helping birth a cow!" He grinned so widely you'd think he was the one who'd given birth. His smile only fueled my anger.

My father had seen the look on my face and diplomatically disappeared—or maybe he'd run for cover.

"Did you name her Princess, your highness?" I had no idea what his title was, and I didn't care. He'd lied to me.

Nick looked like he'd just eaten an unripe grape.

"When were you going to tell me?" I demanded. "After I made a fool of myself over you?"

When he didn't answer, I turned and ran into the barn, leaving Nick standing in the snow, his mouth open in shock.

CHAPTER 9

Our barn still had a hayloft, although we hadn't stored hay there in years due to fire danger. Over the years it had become a repository for extra tack, tools, and old furniture Mom had replaced but that Dad thought was too good to throw out.

That's where I headed, up the steep steps and toward the back of the loft. I'd been coming to the loft since I was a little girl to nurse my hurts and cry when I needed to, and I headed for my favorite old couch, a relic from the 1940's, dark red velvet worn bare in spots and horsehair cushions that never seemed to go flat.

Before I could reach my refuge, though, I felt a hand on my arm, and the next thing I knew, Nick spun me around, and his mouth crashed down on mine. I cried out with surprise, but I couldn't pull away. I was buried in Nick's arms, his warmth enveloping me, and my body refused to do anything but swoon into his. A little voice in the back of my head demanded that I pound on his chest, pull myself out of his embrace and stick to my indignant fury, but somehow my hands crept up and around his neck.

I felt his hot breath on my face, and my eyes closed, my lips parted, absent any thought of my own. This time, when he took my mouth, it wasn't tentative or even particularly gentle. Nor was my response. I opened to him completely, pulling his head down to give him better access, as wave after wave of sensation rippled through my body.

It wasn't enough. I found myself tugging at his jacket, reaching for the buttons on his shirt, needing the feel of his skin, the warmth of him.

Nick needed no encouragement. He picked me up as if I were light as goose down and laid me on the red velvet sofa. Within minutes we were naked on the old horsehair davenport, revealing the mysteries of one another's bodies. Although I'd never seen him lift anything heavier than a full tray of dirty dishes, his body was solid and well-muscled, with a slight sprinkling of dark hair on his chest.

His tongue teased my lips, my tongue, then reached deep into my mouth. When he drew back, my eyes opened, and as I looked up, it felt like he were reaching into my soul. I wanted to look into his sapphire eyes forever, but my body would wait no longer. I needed more, and I grabbed his gorgeous body and pulled him to me, wrapping my legs around his hips.

The feel of him entering me was like nothing I'd ever experienced. If every lock has a key, Nick was my key. And then I couldn't think at all. Me, Emily Miller, sensible girl, was overtaken by pure sensation. It pulled me under, and I barely heard my own gasps and moans of pleasure, my pleas for more. When my body convulsed around him, it was like nothing I'd ever felt. I lost all control, begged him to give me everything as I gave myself fully to him. I felt his seed fill me, hot and satisfying, as I'd never felt before.

Afterwards, we collapsed in a tangle, both of us oblivious to the cold as we gasped in one another's arms. When I finally came down from the aftershocks of my bliss, I opened my eyes to find Nick watching me with concern.

He reached out and touched my wet cheek, scooped up what I realized was a tear, and licked it off his finger.

"Oh, Em," he said. "I'm so sorry I hurt you. I didn't mean to deceive you. I actually thought you were the one playing a joke on me at first, pretending you didn't know. And then I grew to like that you treated me like a normal person. By then, it was too late to tell you without causing embarrassment."

"Yeah," I said, hiding my face in his shoulder. "It is too late for that."

He stroked my hair and leaned down to kiss my shoulder. "I was selfish, I know that. But it was just so nice to be with someone who liked me for myself, not my titles. I was planning to tell you here, maybe take you for a hike in the mountains…"

It felt like a huge, ugly snake was unwinding from around my heart. My tears had nothing to do with his status or the fact that he'd lied. They were for the way he made me feel. "That's not why I'm crying," I admitted.

"Then why… What is it, my beautiful Em?" Nick looked confused, but his legs remained entwined with mine.

I had no idea what to tell him, but as another wave of emotions washed over me, my heart spoke. "It's just that I've never, it's never…"

He pulled back, looking horrified. "You mean this is your first time?"

I cut him off. "No, not that. It's just that I've never done *that*."

Nick collapsed back into my arms, this time rolling me toward the sofa back so his weight wouldn't crush me. "Thank God. You had me going there for a minute."

"I've never felt like that," I said.

He looked deep into my eyes. "It's never been like that for me, either."

He leaned in and kissed me gently and deeply, and my fears melted. At last, he pulled back, his eyes gleaming with mischief. "And not just because we're in a barn."

We lay like that, pressed against each other, until the chill of the hayloft began to penetrate my body. Nick didn't seem affected, but I began shivering, and he quickly pulled me to my feet and helped me dress. Not sure that I was warm enough, he wrapped his jacket over my shoulders.

"Should we head back to the house and the furnace?" he asked.

"You can, but I still have chores."

"Chores?" Nick looked perplexed.

"Bessie just calved, so she's fine, but Boots still needs to be milked. After our little scene downstairs, I doubt Dad is about to come out here and do it. And in case you think you're off the hook, I'm still upset about you not telling me who you are."

He hung his head. "We can talk about it more, if you like."

"Not now, but I have questions for later, Mister. Don't think I've forgotten that you lied to me about who you were all that time. For now, I have to attend to Boots. You can go up to the house."

I climbed down the ladder and headed toward the milking stand, stopping for a bit to admire the new calf and give Bessie scratches, praise, and a couple of windfall apples from a bin we kept for that purpose.

I was surprised to see that Nick was following me.

"They really are beautiful creatures," he said. "And I've never seen a birth before." We watched little Princess bumping at her mom's full udders and suckling.

"Most people haven't seen a calf born," I said. "You're kind of blessed. She bumps Mom like that to let her know it's time to let her milk come down."

"Makes sense," Nick agreed, his arm around my shoulders.

Boots was a few stalls down, far enough away that she wouldn't be frightened if something had gone wrong with the birth. She had a simple halter, and I led her to the milking stand, grabbed a big bucket, and sat on a stool beside the stand.

Despite my telling him to go to the house, Nick was right beside me. "I thought you attached some kind of machine to them to get the milk."

"You do if you have a dozen or more and a dairy operation going, but we only have two cows, and they're part of the family. Would you like a machine grabbing your teats and squeezing the milk out?"

He grimaced. "Point taken. So how do you do it?"

I grinned. I just couldn't help myself. "Watch and learn."

Some people didn't care as much about their livestock as I did, but they didn't know what they were missing. I started by scratching Boots behind the ears, then rubbing her sides a bit, and finally took a few minutes to push gently on her udder, mimicking the actions of a calf. Then I gently grabbed two teats and began milking gently. The pattern was hypnotic and familiar from my childhood, and I laid my head against her flank milking until the two milk bags were empty.

Nick hadn't left, though I wasn't sure why. I looked at him questioningly.

"Do you think I could try?" he asked.

I looked at Boots, who seemed completely at ease with his presence. "Sure, but follow my instructions exactly."

"Of course."

I got up off the stool, and told him to scratch Boots' head, then pet her side. He followed my instructions to the letter.

"Now, sit down on the stool, and take a couple of minutes to rub the side of her udders that are still full. Give them a few gentle bumps."

"No problem."

I was pleased that Boots seemed to like him.

"Now, take one teat in each hand, and begin to milk her. Gently pull one teat, which will release the milk, then empty it into the bucket by squeezing your fingers together, top to bottom."

"Well, what do you know, the prince of England is milking a cow in my barn," I marveled.

Nick chuckled and shook his head.

Joking aside, I was astonished at how quickly he got the rhythm, and far quicker than I would have expected, he had emptied the other side of her udder. I checked to be sure she was properly cleaned out and released her from the stanchion.

Nick looked ridiculously proud of himself as he stood there holding the pail of milk. He absolutely beamed when I gave him a scoop of molasses-soaked grain to feed her. It was so cute I had to resist the urge to pinch his cheeks.

"What do we do with the milk?" he asked when Boots had finished devouring the grain and receiving more head scratches.

"You," I said, "Bring the bucket into the house for Mom to deal with. And remember, you still owe me a lot more explanation."

CHAPTER 10

Nick carried the bucket of rich, steaming milk into the kitchen without spilling a drop. It was hard to stay mad at a man who was so tickled at milking his first cow. Maybe tomorrow I'd show him how to give the barn cats a treat by squirting a little into their open mouths. Today we'd set out a dish of milk for them before coming in, but that wasn't the same.

It would be fun, something he'd remember forever. But then it struck me that, while all that was true, it was different for him. This was like a vacation at a dude ranch, not an introduction to a way of life. I drooped a little at that but reminded myself that I hadn't been looking for a husband when I met him, and I wasn't ready for one now. What was wrong with enjoying the present?

And the present was a cozy house with a fire roaring and Christmas music playing quietly from the stereo. Nick set the bucket, which weighed around fifty pounds, on the kitchen counter with no apparent effort. He might not have done an honest day's work in his life, at least not what we considered work out here, but he was strong enough for all practical purposes, despite the beautifully manicured nails.

Mom walked in and gave me a cautious smile. She hated conflict almost as much as she hated seeing any of her family hurting. I returned a bright, reassuring smile. It was Christmas, after all. No need to spread my confusion to the rest of the clan.

"What should I call you, Mrs. Miller?" Nick asked politely.

"Well, dear," she said. "Everyone around here, John included, calls me Mom. You might as well do the same. I'd stick with Mr. Miller for her dad, though, until he tells you different."

"Thank you… Mom." I couldn't quite read the look on Nick's face, but I had the oddest feeling that he was blinking back tears. Maybe the Queen of England didn't go by Mum.

"Of course, dear," Mom said, laying a gentle hand on his arm. "We're so happy to have you hear for the holidays. Everyone should be with family during Christmas, even if they can't be with their own."

"What do we do with all this milk?" Nick asked, peering into the bucket and clearing his throat.

"It isn't as much as you might think, with three growing girls, pigs, cats, and dogs," Mom said with a smile. "But first, have you tasted the fresh milk?"

Nick looked doubtfully at the bucket and shook his head. "Don't you have to do something to it before it's edible?"

"Not if your pastures and barns are clean," she assured him. "I sell fresh unpasteurized milk to half a dozen moms in the area." She grabbed a spoon, gave it a good stir, and scooped out a small glass for Nick.

For the first time, he hesitated. "You're sure?"

"Emily never drank anything else 'til she went away to college. I don't think the English are allergic to real milk, either."

Nick looked at me for reassurance, but I just gave him a challenging smile. "Your little Princess out there is going to drink it. Are you scared a tiny newborn calf can handle it better than a big strapping man?"

"Of course not." He took a tentative sip, then another, and finally finished the small glass. "Well, Mum, I can't deny that's good stuff."

"Yes, Boots and Bessie are both Jerseys, and their milk has a high butterfat content. That's why the first thing we do is separate the milk and cream, because taking off a bunch of the cream gives us normal milk, and also butter and whipping cream." Mom explained. "You want to watch how we do it?"

"Of course."

She reached for the bucket, but Nick grabbed it. "If I'm going to watch, I might as well help," he said. "Where to?"

Mom led him to the back porch, where we had an old-fashioned cream separator bolted to the floor. Dad had offered to get an electric model hundreds of times, but Mom insisted she liked the antique model. And, frankly, the big job about separating milk wasn't turning the crank for a couple of minutes, it was cleaning the parts afterwards. The double dishwashers in the kitchen took care of that.

"This machine uses centrifugal force to separate the milk and cream," Mom explained. "You see, cream is lighter than milk, and when I crank the handle, the lighter cream comes out the higher spout, and the milk the other."

I smiled as I recalled her explaining the same thing to me. I was eight at the time.

"Can I give it a go?" Nick asked.

"Sure," Mom agreed. "Just get a nice steady rhythm going. It only takes a few minutes."

He was properly amazed at the thick, heavy cream accumulated in one bowl and the milk poured out into a larger pot.

"Now, we put the girls to work," she said, "Lizzie, Jenny!"

The girls appeared promptly, glancing shyly at Nick. "Yes, Mom?"

"It's Christmas Eve. The pigs are expecting their treat, and you're going to give everyone their Christmas Eve dinners. Kibbles soaked in cream for the barn cats, milk, potatoes and apples for the pigs, and for the horses, apples and carrots and their usual ration of grain."

The girls dashed off to distribute the special Christmas Eve meal to the livestock. It was a tradition that everyone got a special treat for the holidays. Even the beef cows, who stayed close to the barn when the weather got cold, were given a double ration of molasses-rich grain, though it was distributed by front-loader, as there were always a couple hundred beef cows on the ranch.

As a family that valued tradition, even if we'd only recently invented it, we generally had either beef roast or an exotic meat, such as deer or elk, for Christmas Eve dinner. This year, knowing that Nick was coming for the holidays, Mom had adjusted the menu to give him a taste of America.

We had roast beef for the main course with mashed potatoes and brown gravy on the side. She added grilled corn and a salad with native greens, wild onions and cranberries, with a slightly sweet, creamy dressing. Dessert was wonderful as well, a cobbler that melded blueberries, blackberries, and other berries with nuts, in a creamy base with a crunchy topping. Heaven on a plate.

Nick insisted on helping set the table and load one of the dishwashers even though my sisters and mother tried to stop him, telling him that was no job for a prince.

"Not my first time washing dishes, is it, Em?" he asked, giving me a conspiratorial wink across the room that made me forget I was mad at him.

I watched in amused delight as he took over what was traditionally my job. A few minutes before dinner was served, crept over and slid an arm around my waist. He leaned down and whispered in my ear. "What is the proper attire for this meal?"

"Pajamas," I answered promptly. "Preferably Christmas pajamas."

"But I don't have any Christmas pajamas," he said, looking close to panic. "I prefer sleeping in the buff, but of course when I'm a guest, I bring along some..."

"So, go change," I said. "You couldn't be expected to know the 'proper attire,' so just wear what you have. Seriously, my family doesn't care."

He looked embarrassed. "They're a bit... Fancy. Satin, you know."

Guilty that I'd forgotten to tell him this part of the tradition, I gave him a reassuring smile. "Let me see what I can do."

Dad had not been idle while the cooking progressed. He'd made sure the fireplace was stoked to keep the house warm in the Montana night and put the color cones in a basket for everyone to add to the fire. A whole set of Christmas stories, from Dicken's *Christmas Carol* to Dr. Seuss's *The Grinch*, as well as a couple of lesser-known Christmas stories were laid out on the coffee table. He was lighting the candles in the family room when I found him.

"We have a little problem, Dad," I said with a smile. "I forgot to tell Nick to bring some Christmas pajamas."

His brow wrinkled for a minute, then he grinned. "He's a little thinner than me, but I think I have a pair that'll do. I never wore 'em because your Aunt Linda gave them to me and they're a little on the long side. Can't be tripping on the stairs and breaking my neck when we're snowed in."

"That's great, Dad. Should I tell him to come see you?"

He prodded the roaring fire in the fireplace before turning for the stairs. "Imagine," I heard him mutter as he headed up. "A prince wearing my pajamas!"

I headed back to the kitchen, where Nick was still assisting my mom, apparently learning how to make whipped cream. I couldn't imagine a world in which you didn't learn that by the time you were ten, but I was sure he couldn't imagine a world where I trekked into a snowy wilderness to find my birthday present.

"Nick," I whispered.

"Yes?" He stepped away from Mom and raised an eyebrow. "Did you find something suitable for the occasion?"

"Yes, my Dad has some he's never even worn that he can let you use."

"Brilliant!" He excused himself from helping Mom, and I told him where to find Dad.

I finished helping Mom with the final touches to the meal, and then slipped upstairs to put on my new Christmas pajamas, which I had to admit, were a bit more risqué than usual. Thanks to the internet, I'd been able to find sugar-plum fairy pajamas, complete with gauzy wings and a rather low neck. I'd ordered them after inviting Nick home for the holidays, though I was sure he wasn't the reason I'd chosen such a pair.

My family was the only one I knew that actually had a dinner bell, and it rang just as I finished my make-up. You couldn't be a sugar-plum fairy without rosy cheeks, long lashes and kissable pink lips, after all.

As was my usual practice, I waited at the top of the stairs while the rest of the family filed in. Not surprisingly, Mom had dressed as a rather thin Mrs. Claus, and the girls were elves—they almost chose elves or reindeer. Dad descended the stairs in an odd costume that I finally identified as Father Christmas. Even old Joe was dressed up, wearing a rather lopsided pair of antlers and a big Christmas bow. He wasn't the only family dog, but he was the only one who rated a costume.

I waited for Nick to appear. After what seemed like a long pause, he stepped out of the guest room in a very fuzzy brown onesie, complete with hoofs in the feet, a respectable pair of antlers, and a battery-powered red nose.

I couldn't help myself. I burst into laughter. He stalked over, grasped my arms gently, and gave me a severe look. "You might want to be careful with an outfit like that, or there will be some serious reindeer games going on under your parents roof this Christmas."

I giggled. "Promises, promises."

We descended the stairway to Christmas Eve dinner, arm in arm, Nick's battery-powered red nose flashing on and off to guide our way, my wings fluttering.

Dinner was a pleasant, if extended, event with lots of joking, story-telling, and Mom's long-winded descriptions of every dish and how they fit into the American story. By the time we got to dessert, I was stuffed and sleepy, but Nick was eating up Mom's every word.

After dinner, we all retired to the family room to gather around the fireplace and take turns reading from our favorite Christmas stories. Funny, I'd never noticed how set in our Christmas traditions we were until there was an outsider there to observe. I felt a little self-conscious as I imagined Nick's royal life, how fancy his rituals and ceremonies were compared to ours.

Dad had the fire burning brightly by the time we got to the family room. My sisters threw the color cones onto the fire to make the flames all different colors. Between the firelight, the candles, and the twinkling, tall fir tree my parents had cut from off the back acres and hauled in for the season, the room was lit with a cozy, warm glow.

My parents settled into their chairs while my sisters took the sofa with a couple of the family dogs. That left the love seat for Nick and me. I smelled a set-up, but I didn't challenge them on it. In truth, I wanted any excuse to cuddle up to my handsome prince in front of the fire.

The Miller family tradition now called for us to enjoy our favorite winter drinks while we read—hot cocoa for the girls; Dad was a bourbon man; and Mom loved her homemade eggnog. I was still searching for my perfect Christmas drink. The sideboard at the back of the room held an insulated pot of hot chocolate, a variety of liquors, a punch bowl of eggnog, most of which would go to waste if experience had taught me anything, and a steaming bowl of something I didn't recognize. It smelled of cinnamon.

Nick's eyes lit up when he saw it, and he broke into a broad smile. "Mum! You heated up the wassail I brought."

Mom glowed at the praise, though it felt weird to me, hearing Nick calling her Mom. Well, that was what she'd told him to do.

"What's wassail?" I asked.

"It's a traditional English Christmas punch, with a base of apple cider," Nick said. "I brought some for your family, but I didn't expect you to put it out with your own favorites."

"It's your favorite," Mom said with a gentle smile. Her unspoken words, that he was part of the family, made my heart glow like his reindeer nose.

He scooped up a full cup for himself and raised his eyebrows at me. "You up for giving it a go? I did try out fresh milk, after all."

"What's in it?" I asked, curious but not as hesitant as he'd been with the milk.

"Allspice, cinnamon, nutmeg, cloves, and ginger, plus plenty of booze."

"I'll give it the old college try." To tell the truth, I'd been on board when I smelled cider and cinnamon.

The drink was delicious, and I put aside all of my worries about Nick's lineage and failure to tell me about it for the future. We cuddled up on the loveseat and listened as each family member read all or their favorite part of a Christmas story.

As usual, Mom started with her favorite, *T'was the Night Before Christmas*. Dad always found a new version of the *Rudolph the Red-Nosed Reindeer* story, and Lizzie chose to sing, "I want a hippopotamus for Christmas." We all laughed and applauded and refilled our glasses, our cheeks pink and eyes sparkling from the merriment.

Then Jenny, the youngest and a budding writer, had found a poem by T.S. Elliot called "Journey of the Magi." It started out as a lovely story of the Magi's trip to see the baby Jesus but ended more mystically. She ended with a flourish as we all sat in silence, ruminating over her words. I felt the richness of meaning in our Christmas ceremonies, our celebration of love.

I also knew I needed to lighten the mood, or it would be a very weird Christmas Eve.

I started by asking Nick if he wanted to help me toss a few color-flame pinecones into the fire. Treated with chemicals that burned different colors, the fireplace was suddenly filed with pink, green and blue flames again. Then I held up my favorite book. "That was a lovely poem, but no one can outdo the true poet of the last century," I joked. "Dr. Seuss!"

Armed with the book to remind me of all the words and another cup of warm, cinnamon-scented wassail, I lifted the mood with *How the Grinch Stole Christmas*.

By the end of the tale, everyone was laughing again.

After a bit of chit-chat, we all looked at Nick. His arm had been around me all evening, and though he seemed happy and comfortable, he'd hardly spoken.

"Well?" Jenny prompted. "It's your turn, your majesty. Tell us a Christmas story!"

He looked uncomfortable. "I'm not sure I remember any."

I was content to let him off the hook, but the girls weren't. They fussed, whined, and cajoled until he finally conceded.

"All right, but I don't have the book. I may not get it all right." After being assure that no one cared, he refilled our cups of wassail and began.

"This is a story called the *Tailor of Gloucester*, by Beatrix Potter, if you ever want to read the whole thing."

The girls' eyes were glued to him as he started the simple, heartwarming story. The story featured a tailor who had to rely on a group of mice for help in making a waistcoat for the Mayor by his Christmas wedding. Unfortunately, the tailor had freed a group of mice from his cat, and the cat hid a piece of the unfinished waistcoat for revenge. The tailor falls ill, and can't remake the missing piece, and the mice pitch in to finish for him. The cat eventually gave back the piece he stole, and everyone ended up happy for Christmas.

The girls were enthralled and begged Nick for more details, which I suspected he made up to please them. I found myself tearing up, whether from the story, the wassail, or the company, I really couldn't say. All I knew was that despite Nick's deception, I found myself in danger of falling head over heels for him. At any rate, this was shaping up to the best, most memorable Christmas Eve ever.

We all headed upstairs for bed shortly thereafter, slightly tipsy and glowing with the joy of the season, of the love and family around us to warm us through the cold night.

CHAPTER 11

As I made my way down the hall to my childhood bedroom, I forced myself not to look back at Nick. If I looked back, I wouldn't be able to stop myself from inviting him in, and then....

There was no question what would happen next, despite the fact that this had been my room since I was a baby, and my parents were down the hall one way and my little sisters the other. Home had always been separate from the feelings I had for Nick, so I'd never even considered the possibility of inviting a man into my room. But now, those feelings wouldn't leave. I stripped off my Christmas PJs and climbed between the sheets, knowing the fluffy white comforter Mom preferred would keep my nakedness warm as toast. Or hot as hot sauce, I decided as images of Nick simply wouldn't leave my mind.

I don't know how long I laid there, trying all the tricks I'd learned to go to sleep. None of them worked. Not even close. I needed a good, cold shower or maybe an ice-cube bath. I couldn't quite bring myself to go that route in the middle of winter, so I kept trying to sleep.

It was useless. The more I tried to sleep, the more thoughts demanded attention. The more I recalled the feel of Nick's lips on mine, the feel of him pushing inside of me, opening places I didn't know I had, filling me and freeing me and making me forget everything except the simple, amazing moment of connection, of release. For the very first time, feeling that melding, that surrender I'd only heard about, until there was only pure sensation, pure communion.

I refused to use the word love.

Somehow, I shook the feeling off and stopped myself from running down the hall into the arms I longed for. Instead, I fanned my face for a moment and scolded myself. It was ridiculous to get so emotional about Nick. I should be happy that I'd finally learned the difference between good sex and the kind I'd had before.

Nick would be gone in a year or two, no matter what happened now, and I would be left here in my beautiful mountains.

And that was right. Really, it was. He had his duties, his family, far away from my life. My life was here, and that wouldn't change. No one and nothing would shake my need to saddle Iris and ride her into the mountains with a hunk of cheese, a ripe pear, and a bottle of wine in my saddlebags, along with a few carrots and apples, two with a drizzle of caramel. One for me, because I love caramel apples, and one for Iris, because caramel tastes a little like molasses, and horses love molasses.

Outside the window, I saw a few snowflakes begin to fall. I was too old to think I'd miss Santa if I stayed up, and sleep was clearly beyond me, so I decided on the next best thing.

Climbing out of bed, I started with my feet, putting on a pair of heavy wool socks. Then, a pair of thermal underwear, bottom and top, my clothes. After tiptoeing down the hall so I wouldn't wake anyone, I padded down to the mud room and pulled on a fleece-lined snowsuit, my favorite snow hat, complete with bunny ears and a nose cover, and my boots and gloves.

The mud room had a back door, but it made an awful, loud squeak. I made my way back to the living room and slipped through the French doors to the glassed-in porch. The porch door was silent as a snowdrift.

I was almost to the outside door when a small sound made me pause. Turning around, I realized that Nick was sitting on the porch, bundled up almost as well as I was. "Going somewhere?" he asked.

"I couldn't sleep," I admitted, hoping he couldn't see my blush, couldn't guess that he was the one coming between me and sweet dreams.

"Likewise," he said. "Where are you off to, Miss Em?"

"I thought I'd take a walk."

"Care for company?"

Darn. How was that going to help me sleep? Or think?

I looked him up and down. "Not in those shoes," I said, seeing that he still had his slippers on, despite his otherwise warm outfit. Maybe I was saved, after all.

"I have snow boots in the back hall if you'll give me a moment."

He was gone before I could think of a better objection, and back with an extra coat and boots before I could catch my breath.

I didn't really mind the company, though I knew time alone meant we'd likely have to hash out our earlier disagreement. He opened the porch door for me, and as I stepped out into the silent, white wonderland, he took my hand.

"Where to?" he asked.

I thought for a moment. "Do you want a nice walk in the snow or an adventure?"

"I'm always up for an adventure," he said, smiling down at me. "That's why I'm here in America."

My mind went to the Secret Cave, the only place I'd never shown anyone, not even my sisters. They had never mentioned a cave, so I'd always clung to the hope that they hadn't discovered it, and it was still my secret. I hadn't been there in at least ten years, but I knew the way, and once there, I'd know whether anyone else had found it.

"Are you warm enough for a mile or two walk?" I asked.

"Actually, I'm sweating in here."

"I have just the place," I said. "Somewhere no one else knows about."

He gave me a small, dimpled smile. "I would be honored."

We made a short stop at the barn to pick up a couple of flashlights, though we really didn't need them with the snow lighting up the night. I checked to be sure I had my cellphone, and that it was charged. There was a difference between adventurous and foolhardy, especially after dark.

The night was cloudless, cold and dry, and the stars and even the planets sparkled in the way they can only in Montana. Nick's warm fingers enveloped my gloved hand, but he let me lead, the flashlights off. Sitting on the porch, it was easy to think of the still, snowy landscape as silent, but that was far from the reality.

Every step we took produced a lovely crunch, and our breath made a gentle whispery sound, and filled the air with smoky ice crystals. If you stopped for a moment, you might hear winter birds murmuring their night sounds, a pine tree dumping its load of snow onto the ground below, or even the distant howl of a wolf or a coyote.

Every now and then, I had to stop and listen. I'd needed this, and I couldn't bear to miss a precious moment.

"Are we lost?" Nick asked as we stopped for the fourth time.

I chuckled, feeling better every minute. Oh, how I had needed this connection with my world, my life. "Not at all," I replied. "I'm just stopping to enjoy the night sounds. We'll be there in a few minutes."

His chuckle was deep and warm. "I was getting a little nervous, I admit."

"See that dark spot up ahead?" I asked. "That's our destination."

"I'll trust you," he said, squeezing my hand gently.

"It'll be worth the walk, I promise," I assured him.

As we covered the last few yards, I wondered why I had decided to bring him here. This was my place, and mine alone. Yet here we were. I had no answers, except that I'd wanted to share it with this man, just as I wanted to share my heart.

I turned on my light, and the entrance was flooded with a golden glow. Every cave is different, and often the entrances are completely uninteresting. A little hole in the dirt, or water running into an opening that seems larger than the outside area. That was not the case here. For whatever reason, the entrance here was rimmed with stalactites and baby stalagmites. Native bushes around it hid it from view, which was why no one had found it. The only reason I had was that Iris had stopped to nibble on the growth one day, and I'd noticed the darkness beyond.

My light shone on glistening snow, ragged local bushes and beautiful crystals, dripping from the ceiling of the chamber. Tiny, damaged stalagmites tried to reach up from the bottom. I felt a pang of guilt. The damaged stalagmites were my fault. I'd come here often as a child.

Leading downward was a pathway, high enough for me to stand upright, although Nick had to bend a bit.

"I call this the Crystal Staircase."

"Beautiful," Nick breathed.

He followed, one hand on my shoulder, as I descended carefully down the limestone pools. It wasn't far, maybe twenty pools, but it was enough. The cave opened up as it joined a small stream, garnished with more stalactites above and various limestone formations all around.

Across the stream, which was small enough to easily step across at this season, there was a widened spot with several formations that would look like benches to a ten-year-old.

I headed for my favorite bench and, turning the light on bright, reached into the dug-out cavern I'd made so many years ago. Everything I'd brought was still there, untouched. A whole bearskin, which Dad had shot before I was born, a heavy wool blanket from the nearby reservation, and half a dozen candles. There were even provisions, although I wasn't sure they were still edible after all these years.

I spread the bearskin on the rock shelf, motioned Nick to join me, and began lighting candles.

"I found this cave when I was little. Even my sisters don't know about it."

"Just me?"

"Just you." I smiled at him, my heart feeling light and melty at the same time.

He made a noise that I couldn't interpret. "How old were you?"

"About ten," I answered. "I'm not sure what else I left here, but I'll check in a minute. However, I did leave snacks." A mischievous smile crept onto my face. Hopefully, he didn't see it.

"Em, No!" Nick sounded concerned. "Anything here has been in this cave for years."

"So?" I asked. "I only left for college three years ago."

"What about mold? What about... worms?"

"Haven't you ever seen Zombinight?" I asked, feeling better than I'd felt all day.

"Zombi what?" Nick's brow wrinkled. He was clearly unacquainted with the vintage film classic.

"Zombinight. It's a classic. We'll watch it tomorrow night, and maybe *The Grinch*. In the meantime, you need to try a Twinkie. I'm not sure, but I don't believe these things have expiration dates. Besides, it's not that old. I discovered it when I was ten, but I've used it as my getaway for years."

I tore a package open and gave it a sniff. Seemed okay. I poked at the sponge cake that cradled the creamy filling. A little firmer than all those years ago, but certainly edible. The greasy, sweet smell screamed for me to take a nibble.

Deciding to toss my fate to the wind, I took a bite. It wasn't bad, maybe a little dried out, but still better than most dorm breakfasts. I offered one to Nick, who recoiled.

After a bit of teasing, he gave in and took a bite, though. His face melted into a look of confusion. "My God, these are delicious. Why don't they sell them in England?"

I chuckled a little. "They probably do. Just not to princes. This is the food of commoners, Nick Lancaster, Crown Prince of England."

"Do you have to call me that?" he asked, his eyes softening.

"I don't have to," I said. "And since it's Christmas, I won't."

"Merry Christmas, sweet Em," he murmured. He leaned in, and after a moment, his lips met mine with heartbreaking tenderness. Like the Grinch, my heart grew ten sizes.

CHAPTER 12

I woke with a start in the darkness with warm arms wrapped around me. The air was chilly and damp, but everything but my nose was snuggly warm. After a moment of disorientation, I realized I must have fallen asleep in the cave with Nick. I looked up to see him smiling down at me, and I had to fight the urge to just snuggle closer and go back to sleep.

That would never do, though. Everyone was up early on Christmas morning, and my absence would cause general hysteria. I wriggled in his arms, trying to shake off the sleep. "How long have I been out?" I mumbled.

"Only an hour or so," he said soothingly. "We'll get back before morning."

I relaxed and let my body wake up at a more respectable pace. "Did you fall asleep, too?"

"No, Em."

"What were you doing, then?"

"Watching you. Watching the little patch of stars through the cave mouth. Thinking."

I desperately wanted to ask him what he'd been thinking about, but I couldn't find the words. Instead, I struggled onto my knees and began tidying up the cave. That made me think of the Little Prince sweeping his volcano, but I didn't mention it. Such an old story, he probably didn't know it.

Nick helped fold the blankets and pick up the Twinkie wrappers. The candles had gone out on their own.

As we climbed up the gentle slope of the cave, my Crystal Staircase, he kept a hand on my waist, presumably in case I slipped. "You know," he remarked as we emerged into the clear, starry night. "Those cake rolls were good, but I don't think that storing them in a cave for years is the best practice."

"I know," I admitted. "I've never tried them after that long, but I couldn't resist. Thanks for being such a good sport. I can't believe the prince of England ate three-year-old cave snacks."

"Next time, we'll bring a picnic. I couldn't bear to lose you to bad Twinkies."

Next time? I wondered what that meant. How could there possibly be a next time for a prince and a would-be teacher?

I pushed the thought away as we walked through the still night. I refused to worry about it anything right now. I was just going to enjoy this perfect, peaceful Christmas morning.

We walked hand in hand back to the house through the still night, the snow crunching gently under our feet, the occasional animal sound breaking through the silence. I let the past and future go, and moved in the moment, our bodies in harmony, spirits in sync.

We opened the back door quietly and shut it with care, shed our outer garments and boots, and tiptoed up the back stairs. At my bedroom door, Nick took my face in his hands and looked into my eyes.

"Good night, my Em," he whispered, right before his lips covered mine. Again, I was lost in pure sensation, a feeling of wholeness I'd never felt with anyone else.

It was Nick who finally pulled away. "Get some sleep, Love. We have a long day tomorrow, I suspect."

He turned and disappeared down the hall, and I stared after him for a long minute.

He'd said, "Love."

Surely, it was just an expression. Wasn't that a common English greeting?

I finally stepped into my bedroom and closed the door, refusing to consider that question any longer. My clothes went into a heap on the floor, and I crawled into my cozy bed, which for the first time, felt too empty. Still, I was asleep almost before my head hit the pillow.

My dreams were warm, fuzzy, and all about Nick.

Daybreak came too early, but I awoke feeling energized and amazingly happy. The excitement of racing downstairs to see what Santa had brought was long gone, but I stretched lazily, enjoying the delicious sensation of being home and full of joy on this special day.

No matter what the future held, today was perfect. I was in my beloved home, surrounded by family, with a man I loved. It was hard to admit, but sometime during the night, in my dreams, I'd come to terms with it. He might break my heart, and it might never work between us, but I couldn't deny the reality. I was in love with Nick Lancaster, first in line for the English throne.

With that thought in mind, I climbed from bed, anxious to see a man with a lot less beard and a lot less white hair than Old Saint Nick.

I always wore red for Christmas as it made me feel festive and went well with my skin and hair. This year, I'd picked out a cute outfit that was a little more feminine than my family was used to. I was sure I would get some teasing from Jenny and Lizzie, but they weren't my intended audience. Hopefully Nick would enjoy it, and my parents wouldn't be scandalized.

To begin, I pulled on a pair of red lace panties and a matching bra—those were for me, not an audience, or so I'd thought at the time of purchase. Then a pair of red and gray brocade harem pants, heavy enough to keep me warm in this climate but hanging low on the hips, a look I loved but only occasionally dared to wear. My red top had long puffy sleeves and a rather low neck and ended two inches above where the low-rise pants hung.

A touch of red lip gloss, a French braid with a few Christmas rosebuds tucked in, and a brass python bracelet curled around one arm completed the costume. Our family had a tradition of dressing up for Christmas, I just hoped Dad wouldn't wrinkle his brow in disapproval at my exposed midriff.

When I got downstairs, I saw Lizzie had decided on a Christmassy Tinkerbell costume, and for unknown reasons, Jenny was dressed as a bright red dragon, complete with tail. They were both awake and staring at the Christmas tree as if they had x-ray vision. Even though we were all too old for Santa, the warmth and joy of the day swept over me when I saw the twinkling lights on the tree and the neatly wrapped boxes beneath. My kooky sisters made the picture complete, almost bringing a tear to my eye. The smell of freshly baked bread mixed with the faint scent of the needles on the tree, and the sounds of Christmas music drifted from the stereo in the kitchen.

I headed that way to help Mom, who had decided that this was the Christmas to dress as a Christmas elf—green leggings, cute hat, the whole works. She was busy cutting the breakfast rolls: yeast dough she'd made last night and set to rest, rolled out thin and wound into pinwheels. There were three rolls, one cinnamon, one chocolate frosting, and the third her homemade orange marmalade.

We hugged and wished each other Merry Christmas, complimented each other's costumes, and began working on the buffet. I set out mimosas, sausages from the local butcher, and a giant pile of scrambled eggs with red and green pepper bits, onions, and on top, a pile of white, fluffy cheese. Mom called her eggs "snow on the mountain." Again, I realized that our customs and traditions might seem silly to a prince, and I steeled myself for his possible disapproval.

Still, this was us. Love me, love my family.

Lizzie managed to pry herself away from the presents under the tree to check out the buffet table and announced, petulantly, "There aren't any rolls! And what are we supposed to drink?"

"Calm down, Munchkin," Mom said. "The rolls are about to be frosted. And your drinks are coming."

With my help, Mom brought out another pitcher of orange juice and a bottle of sparkling grape juice. She also had a dish of skewers, umbrella on one end, and maraschino cherries and pineapple chunks on the other. "Don't get into them until everyone is here."

Nick chose that moment to come downstairs, wearing what was probably proper English Christmas breakfast attire. Dark slacks, a long-sleeved shirt, and a sweater—no tie, thank goodness. He looked so out of place.

I didn't care. He looked good enough to eat.

He surveyed the buffet and looked at Mom. "You must never tell my mother, but this is the best-looking breakfast I've seen in years."

Mom beamed. "We do this every Christmas morning. The rest of the time it's just eggs, meat, bread, and fruit."

Dad came in with an armload of wood for the fireplace. "The cows are milked, and all the animals have had their Christmas breakfasts. Is it time for me to eat?"

"In a moment, Dear," Mom said, putting the final drizzle of icing on the rolls. "After you get rid of that wood, why don't you take these to the buffet?"

Her smile was dazzling.

Dad gave a deep, theatrical sigh. "If you think you can't manage…"

"Well, I thought you'd want butter and marmalade, and a few other little treats…"

I hardly noticed them, since they went through the same routine every year, but Nick was grinning broadly. He followed my dad into the living room.

Mom turned to me. "How's it going, Dear? He seems so charming. So much better than that last one."

"He's wonderful," I agreed. "But I have to be realistic. Where can it go? I'm not cut out to live in London."

"I know you think your soul is here, and it always will be, but your body can be where your heart is." She looked at me soberly. "You can always come back here, for as long as you want, but it's not an either-or choice. Wherever you go, a piece of your heart will be here, ready when you come back.

Don't be foolish. You don't have to choose between love and family."

Completely stunned by Mom's words, I gathered up homemade jams and marmalades, sweet butter from Bessie, and my favorite, a tray of smoked salmon with capers and cucumbers, and headed for the buffet.

Breakfast itself was casual and protracted. Everyone started with a plate of their favorite foods, but once that first plate was empty, everyone went back for more of whatever they wanted. I watched my sisters packing in the sweet rolls and sausage, not to mention the kid-mosas.

After breakfast, we all settled around the living room and opened gifts. The embers from the Yule log still glowed in the fireplace, putting off a gentle heat. Strains of soft music floated in from the kitchen, and my heart swelled with love for my family. Just being there was the greatest gift.

My Christmas gifts were like a whole-semester care package, which was just what I wanted. My sisters' gift to me was more surprising. Before presenting it to me, Jenny and Lizzie had an extended conference behind the Christmas tree. Finally, they emerged, and picked up two packages, which had obviously been wrapped with great care.

Jenny held her present out first. It wasn't heavy, but the shape was strange. For once I was mystified.

"Be careful when you open it," Jenny cautioned somberly. "It's fragile."

"I promise," I assured her, and began peeling off the excessive amount of tape they had used to wrap it. I finally got it untangled from the Scotch tape, paper and ribbons, and was holding my gift. I hate to admit it, because I had no idea what it was. Almost weightless, mainly shades of green, it looked rather like a psychedelic bird's nest made of netting, feathers, flowers and ribbon. "It's... Lovely," I said, turning it over.

"It's a fascinator," Nick said, lighting up. "And a beautiful one. I love the greens, they will go perfectly with Em's hair."

My sisters exploded into an eruption of excitement, shrieking, giggling, and dancing around the Christmas tree.

I slowly figured out that I was looking at a hat, British style. I tried to imagine wearing the odd little bird's nest in public, but I couldn't. Still, these were my sisters, my little chicks.

"Yes, the color is perfect for me!" I exclaimed, deciding that my sisters' feelings were more important than anything. Besides, it really was a great color.

"Try it on! Try it on!" the girls shrieked.

"But my hair…" I protested, laughing.

Nick slid onto the loveseat beside me, reaching around my neck to begin undoing my French braid. I tried to ignore the warm and wonderful feeling of his hands on my neck, my hair…

I wanted to sigh and close my eyes and melt, my breathing beginning to pick up speed.

He leaned close and whispered, "Remember, your sisters are watching us, and your parents…"

That stiffened my spine and brought me back to reality. "Thanks."

"You're welcome." His arrogant grin made me think he knew exactly the effect he had on women.

He fluffed my freed hair a couple of more times and producing a couple of hairpins which he used to attach the fascinator at a jaunty angle. He sat back and looked at me and gave me a cocky little smile. "You look quite fetching, Emily Miller."

"So what's the second present?" I asked, turning away in embarrassment.

Lizzie timidly approached Nick and handed him a long, slim box wrapped in white tissue paper with a Christmas-red ribbon. "We figured she might need these," she said shyly.

Nick handed me the box and waited while I opened it. It was a pair of gloves the color of the lightest feather in the fascinator. They were long, almost to the elbow. Almost before I knew it, Nick had taken the gloves out of the box and helped me into them. They were nothing like the gloves I wore to the barn in the winter. That's all I could say about them. They really were way too fancy for me, but my sisters were awed by the sight of me in a bright green fascinator, a rather racy blouse, and elegant, green gloves. They were probably picturing me being swept away to a palace by my prince.

Awed isn't the word I'd use for the rest of the audience. Mom, Dad and Nick grabbed their phones and began shooting pics of me. Laughing, I gave in and posed for them—a regal, beauty queen wave, a demure look, and a few others.

The rest of Christmas Day was wonderful as well. Nick chuckled at the girls' gift to him of English Leather cologne, and they seemed to love the cashmere scarf sets he'd gotten them. He'd brought Mom an assortment of English delicacies, teacakes, British toffee and licorice, and a subscription plan to deliver such things for the next 12 months. For Dad, a bottle of expensive-looking Scotch, with an apology.

"I didn't know you were a bourbon man, Sir," Nick said, looking uncomfortable.

Dad grinned and help up the bottle, surveying it with satisfaction. "I'm anxious to expand my tastes," he said with a good-natured chuckle.

I couldn't wait to give Nick the leather vest I'd had custom made for him. He put it on, and I had to admit, he looked downright silly. I tried to hold back my laughter as he tried to do some sort of jig, which he said he thought American cowboys did. My sisters howled and rolled on the floor with laughter, knocking over a candle and almost lighting the dragon costume's tail on fire before they recovered. I gave in and giggled a bit too, but Nick said he loved it and planned to wear it back home, if only to scandalize his mother.

When he was done, he slid into the loveseat with me, pulling me into his arms and insisting I open his gift next. It was a necklace, a Celtic knot design with a beautiful green stone at its center. I swallowed hard as he helped me fasten it around my neck. I hoped it was silver, though it looked more like white gold. He shouldn't have spent that much on me!

"It's beautiful," I murmured, thinking that it was too much, too soon. It also made my gift look like even more of a joke.

The rest of the day passed as was usual—we lounged around, laughed, and ate too much at Christmas dinner. I wished it could be Christmas forever.

Nightfall came too soon, as it always did in Montana winters. As we all bid each other goodnight, I wondered if the connection Nick and I had formed was just the

Christmas magic, or was it something more real? I didn't want to be sensible for once, though, so I didn't let myself ponder it too long. Instead, I basked in the feeling of love I'd had all day, the joy of the holiday, the warmth I always got from family and the way Nick had fit right in, despite his princely status. I lay my hand over the necklace I still wore, smiled, and fell into a peaceful slumber.

CHAPTER 13

A soft knock on my door awakened me. I made some kind of sleep-addled sound as I struggled back to wakefulness, wondering if something was wrong. Nick stepped inside and pulled the door closed behind him before he moved across the room and slipped between the covers with me.

"I couldn't wait any longer, Em," he whispered. "I have to talk to you, to make it right. Can I stay?"

I nodded, and he moved closer and encircled me in his arms.

"I had to tell you again, to make you understand. I never meant to hurt you, and it kills me to think that I did." He pulled me closer and kissed my forehead.

"It's okay," I said. "I'm not mad anymore. I can't hold a grudge for anything."

"It's no excuse, but for once in my life, I wanted to be with someone who liked me for who I am, not *what* I am. I loved the way you looked at me, really *me*. Not as the Duke, not as a prince, not as the first in line to the throne. You saw who I was, and I wanted that so much." His voice caught, and he gently took my face in his hands and stared deep into my eyes.

"I understand," I said, my throat thick with emotion. I leaned forward and kissed him.

"I loved you," he whispered, then repeated a little more firmly, "I love you, Emily."

Looking up into those intense blue eyes, I couldn't deny it. "I think I'm falling in love with you, too, Nick." I said, feeling bad at the way I equivocated. "Falling in love" didn't begin to describe it. I was deep, head-over-heels in love with Nicholas Lancaster, doomed though our love may be.

Nick reached for the necklace he'd given me, the one I had left on because I couldn't imagine taking it off. He held the pendant in his hand and gazed into my eyes. "There's something I didn't tell you in front of your parents. The other name for the Celtic Knot is the Celtic Love Knot, and it stands for true, permanent, abiding love."

I wrapped my arms around his neck, pulling him down until his lips met mine. In time, we were again all tangled up in the covers, trying to shed our pajamas as we touched, and tasted and simply... *Felt*.

This time, there was none of the desperation of that first time, no hurry, no anger. We took our time, exploring each other's bodies, learning responses, and enjoying the difference between love and lust.

Afterwards, as I lay in Nick's arms, I refused to think of the future and what it might hold. We were young. We had time to learn each other better than we knew ourselves. Time to wrestle with what we were meant to do in this world. Most importantly, time to decide. Time to decide if the mountains behind the house were more important than one person inside it. Time to decide whether teaching in England was really so different from doing it here.

Time to decide whether even the true golden flame of love was enough to conquer circumstances, culture, even family. As the saying went, love conquers all.

I fell asleep cozy in Nick's arms and only awakened with the first light of dawn casting patterns on the snowy quilt. I came awake to him gently shaking my shoulder. "We'd probably better wake up now," he murmured, dropping small kisses on my warm cheeks.

I could feel a huge smile spreading over my face. "I suppose, but…" I reached up and gave him a kiss that was more invitation than tease.

"Oh, no, you don't," he said with a laugh, pulling away. "I refuse to be caught by your father in your bed."

The image made me laugh. "I'm with you on that. But maybe just a quick one?"

"Well, if you insist," he said, relenting with a smile that let me know it was all he wanted, too. He rolled onto me, and as he slid inside me, I felt again how right it was, how perfect our bodies fit, the perfection of our union despite all our differences.

"Nick," I breathed as I reached completion. "I love you." To my surprise, I enjoyed the feeling of freedom in speaking what my heart had already known.

"Oh, Em," he whispered, finding his own perfect ending inside me. "My love."

After a few minutes of snuggling, I climbed out of bed and began to look for my robe. Even inside, Montana winters were cold. It didn't take long until we were back in our pj's and robes, and he was standing at my door, ready to head down the hall to his room. As I ran a comb through my very messy hair, I realized he was waiting for something. I turned to face him.

"You better go," I said with a smile, shooing him away.

When he didn't move, I turned back toward him, starting to feel a knot of tension inside me. "What is it?" I asked.

"I have another present for you that I didn't want to give you in front of your parents. In case you said no."

He was acting so strange. I couldn't imagine why, unless he was regretting the things he'd said. "Is everything all right?" I asked.

He fumbled in his pajama pocket and thrust an envelope into my hands. Mystified, I slid a thumbnail under the flap, and the envelope came open. I stopped breathing, because even before taking the stiff paper out of the envelope, I recognized it for an airline ticket. I looked up in shock.

"I thought since we spent Christmas here, you might want to do New Years in England. It might give you a chance to wear the little green bird nest," he said with a crooked smile.

I didn't answer, because I was too busy planting kisses anywhere I could, jumping up and down. Nick loved me, and he wanted to take me home to meet the family. My heart nearly burst with Christmas joy.

"Is that a yes?" he asked, cocking a brow at my over-excitement.

"Yes! Yes! Yes!" My third yes was so loud, I realized my chanced of getting Nick out of the bedroom before my parents woke had gone to zero.

I even didn't care. Despite our differences, Nick wanted to work them out. I was ready, too. Ready to take big chances, to be a girl who was swept away instead of being sensible every moment. Ready to grow, to travel to other countries, to meet a queen. Most of all, I was ready to find out if love really did conquer all.

The End.

AUTHOR'S NOTE

Prince in the Snow is the first (of hopefully many) holiday story set in this world, but it won't be the last! If you'd like to receive updates on future Christmas stories set in Snowy Hollow, please join my special Holiday Newsletter.

You will only hear about Christmas stories, so only a few times a year!

https://landing.mailerlite.com/webforms/landing/i3c9b8